Currents

Currents

Jane Petrlik Smolik

Charlesbridge

Published by Charlesbridge
85 Main Street
Watertown, MA 02472
(617) 926-0329
www.charlesbridge.com

Library of Congress Cataloging-in-Publication Data
Smolik, Jane Petrlik, author.
    Currents / Jane Petrlik Smolik.
        pages cm
    Summary: In 1854, eleven-year-old Bones is a slave in Virginia who
sends a bottle holding her real name and a trinket from her long-lost
father down the James River—the currents carry it far away, ultimately
uniting the lives of three young girls.
    ISBN 978-1-58089-648-1 (reinforced for library use)
    ISBN 978-1-60734-863-4 (ebook)
    ISBN 978-1-60734-900-6 (ebook pdf)
    [1. Slavery—Fiction. 2. African Americans—Fiction. 3. Identity—
Fiction. 4. Social classes—Fiction. 5. Isle of Wight (England)—
History—19th century—Fiction. 6. Great Britain—History—
Victoria, 1837–1901—Fiction. 7. Immigrants—Fiction. 8. Irish
Americans—Fiction. 9. Authorship—Fiction.] I. Title.
PZ7.S66459Cu 2015
813.54—dc23   2014010491

Printed in the United States of America
(hc) 10 9 8 7 6 5 4 3 2 1

Illustrations made with watercolor on Arches watercolor paper
Display type set in Stempel Garamond AS
Text type set in Stempel Garamond AS, ITC Zapf Chancery,
    Metroscript by Alphabet Soup Type Founders,
    and Mostly Regular by Jonathan Macagba
Color separations by Colourscan Print Co Pte Ltd, Singapore
Printed by Berryville Graphics in Berryville, Virginia, USA
Production supervision by Brian G. Walker
Designed by Martha MacLeod Sikkema

To Karen Boss,
for helping me bloom

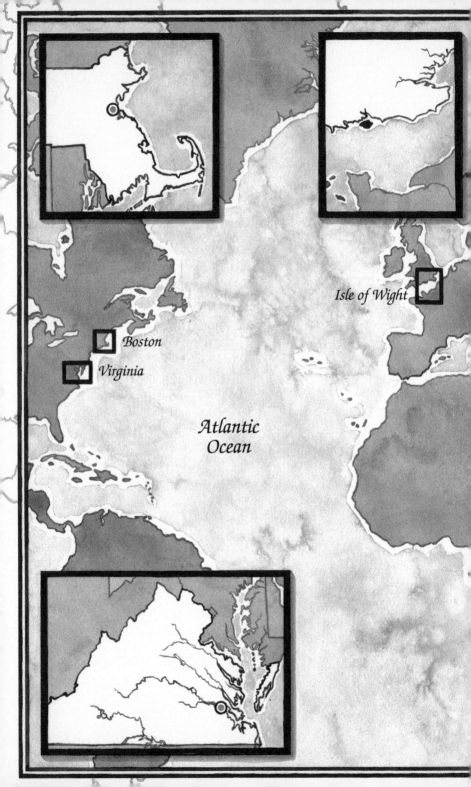

Isle of Wight

Boston

Virginia

Atlantic
Ocean

Contents

BONES

Folks along the James River swore it was because of the tobacco-plant flowers. Queenie, the cook, was certain it was due to all the roses that grew in Old Mistress's gardens. Whatever the reason, the honey that came from Stillwater Plantation's hives was considered the finest in all of Virginia. Friends and neighbors looked forward to a jar at Christmas and on special occasions.

Every other month, Bones covered herself up in the special bee suit that Queenie had made for her and carefully carried her bee-smoker pan to the hives. She slowly filled wide-mouthed bottles with the golden nectar. Every now and again Queenie would slip a jar of the sweet treat to Bones, who would take it home to Granny and Mama.

Bones would always sneak the empty bottle back to the kitchens. Except for the one she saved—that one she kept just for herself.

Chapter One
Virginia, Autumn 1854

Bones was too young to remember the day her pappy had been sold off to another plantation, but she remembered everything about how she learned she was the personal property of another human being.

"Took you so long to sweep the kitchen, you need somethin' else to eat to keep you goin'," fussed Queenie, the cook, as she placed an extra piece of cornbread in front of Bones. The little girl ate it carefully, so as not to drop crumbs on the corncob doll hanging from her neck by a rawhide string.

"You'd better go now and wake up Miss Liza. I suspect you be doin' all sorts of things today. Looks like the sun's gonna be shinin'. And stop jigglin' that foot of yours, or Old Mistress tie you up in a chair again!"

Queenie had been the head cook since Master Brewster bought her years ago and brought her to Stillwater Plantation. She had been born on the Smiths' farm a few miles down the river and had learned as a child to prepare tasty pork, chicken, pies, and fresh greens. Master Colonel Sam Smith sold her for one thousand dollars to the Brewsters solely on her reputation in the kitchen. They sold her on the condition that her new family promised not to beat her, and if she ever acted so badly that she had to have a whupping, her new master would bring her back and drop her off in the yard where he got her.

Every morning when Bones appeared in the kitchen, Queenie was cleaning Master's boots, shoes, and sword, and making his coffee before starting breakfast.

Staring out the Brewsters' kitchen window, Bones had a clear view past the big house and the kitchen gardens to the rows of unpainted cabins. She lived in one of them with her granny and her mother, Grace. Theirs was the farthest one away, and from their door, a weedy dirt path led straight to the fields that sloped gracefully down to the James River. Granny and Mama were field hands, and left every morning before dawn to work the long rows of tobacco, corn, wheat, and cotton. Each cabin had its own garden patch in the back where the slaves were allowed to grow extra food. At night or on Sunday afternoons, they could tend their own rows of cabbage, lima beans, onions, potatoes, black-eyed peas, and collards. If one person had too many collards one week, they would trade with someone who had too many lima beans.

Stillwater was one of a handful of old plantations that sprawled out along Virginia's lower James River. Built with bricks that had been fired on the property and shaded by wide porches framing three sides, it sat at the end of a gravel drive lined with oak trees and mountain laurel. The back porch, which overlooked the river, stretched across the entire length of the house and was held up by eight fluted white pillars. Lounge chairs, tables, and settees were placed neatly about, and magnolias planted around the house brushed against the roof and spilled their fragrance into the soft Virginia air. In the front yard, carefully clipped boxwood hedges surrounded three levels of terraced gardens, built to show off the Mistress's rosebushes.

During the sweltering summers, the river created a welcome breeze through the house. Deep forests at the back of the property provided some of the wood to keep the stoves and fireplaces burning all winter, and the acres of fields kept the slaves busy planting and picking crops. Nine hundred peach trees were planted in a single row like a living fence around one of the backfields. Peach trees grew like weeds in the fertile soil, and field hands cut down one hundred trees a year to use as firewood. In the spring, one hundred new saplings were planted to replace the ones that had been cut.

Master Brewster strolled into the kitchen house and let the door slap shut behind him, tilting his head up to breathe in the sweet fragrance of molasses and chopped peaches.

"Have you woken up Mistress Liza yet?" he asked Bones. His sturdy frame filled the doorway, and his riding boots clacked on the freshly swept floor. As on most large plantations, the kitchen house was a separate building located off to the side to keep the main house cooler and reduce the risk of fires.

"No, Masta," Queenie said, sweet as the shoofly pie she'd begun to assemble. "Bones just goin' up now."

Master Brewster shook the sweat off his large straw hat and leaned down to tug at the girl's braids. Mama fixed them every day to cover her ears that seemed to sprout straight out from her head. But it never worked. Granny said those ears made her special because she could hear extra good.

"And what is this?" He pointed at the old corncob wrapped in a handkerchief hanging from her neck.

"My baby doll," Bones answered.

"Ah! Yes, now I see that." He looked at the plain

corncob, with no face or clothes. "And does your baby doll have a name?"

"Lovely. Her name's Lovely."

"Well, that's a mighty fine name for her," he said with a chuckle. "Is this another baby doll?" he asked, pointing to the peach pit that she rubbed between her fingers.

"No, this here's a heart." She smiled up at him. "My pappy carved it for me and give it to me when I was born. I like how it feels."

"Aha. I see. Well, now you make sure Miss Liza does her reading today," Master instructed. "She can't just play with the animals, pick flowers, and daydream."

Bones carefully balanced the breakfast tray the cook had prepared for her young mistress and walked slowly out the back door, calling out behind her, "Oh yes, I will, Masta Brewster. Don' you worry 'bout that." The s-sound in "Brewster" whistled through the gap between her two front teeth. She went down the short path to the big house and up the back staircase, the one the slaves used. Carrying her mistress's breakfast tray upstairs was the first duty of the day, and sprinkling her bedsheets with refreshing lilac-scented cologne was the last duty at night.

Chapter Two

For the most part, Bones didn't mind her life as Miss Liza's companion. It was certainly much easier being a house slave than a field slave. She had been brought up to the big house when she was five to keep Miss Liza company, and in the six years that followed, the girls had spent countless hours exploring the plantation and playing games. Liza's sister, Jane, was fifteen years old and found plenty of companionship with twin sisters her age who lived on a farm down the road. There was just enough difference in the Brewster girls' ages that Liza needed a playmate of her own. The younger of the Brewster daughters loved to play in the fields and run with the dogs down by the river and on the edge of the woods. She and Bones would gather up pinecones, twigs, fluffy mosses, and little pebbles and build castles with stick bridges and roads that they dug through the soft dirt.

In the afternoons, when the heat drove them back into the big shuttered house, Bones would go to the kitchen and fetch Liza a cold glass of fruity iced tea. Liza always insisted that Queenie make a glass for Bones, too. Then Bones would sit and wave a tasseled fan back and forth over her little mistress while Liza sat with her spelling books and blocks and studied her reading and writing. This was usually done with a great deal of sighing and fiddling, as Liza was not fond of studying. Hanging on Liza's wall was a large, colorful map of the United States of America. Master had stuck a red pin onto the spot to mark the location of Stillwater Plantation, and Liza enjoyed having Bones play student to her geography teacher.

Virginia.

Virginia looked like an old snail trying to slither away from a hungry fox. Liza had taught Bones which way on the map was north, south, east, and west. Just south of Virginia was North Carolina. Long and thin with a tail pointing out west—sneaking into Tennessee. Below that, South Carolina, and then Georgia and Florida.

Bones kept to herself why she was so interested. She reckoned her pappy was in one of those lands, and she planned on finding out where. Her mama and granny didn't know where he'd been sold, but she figured it couldn't be north of here. The Northern states didn't take to slaveholding. If the whispers in the fields were right, the North was going to set all the slaves free or else. She needed to be ready either way. The more she learned about mapping, the better prepared she'd be to find her pappy and reunite him with Mama and Granny. It was going to be a fine day when they were a family again. She had had her plan in place for almost a year now, ever since Liza had begun teaching her the mysteries of the map.

"What do all those lines goin' every which ways mean?" Bones had asked one day, pointing to the letters on some blocks.

"They are the letters of the alphabet, Bones. You've heard Daddy talk about the ABCs. Well, those are the first three letters of the alphabet. See? Here they are. This is an A. The first letter," Liza had said.

Bones had run her finger up one side, slowly down the other and then connected the two in the middle.

"That's an A?" she had asked, eyes wide.

"That is an A. It sure is. And this is a B. The first letter of your name begins with the letter B," Liza had explained.

"These the same lines that's on the map?" she had asked.

"The very same." Liza had drawn two slanted lines

connected at their base. "That's a V. Just like the first letter of Virginia. See here on the map. I taught you where Virginia is."

Bones had looked at her like she had spoken a miracle. It had long ago occurred to Liza that it was more fun playing teacher than simply studying boring books, and in Bones she had an eager student. So afternoons that summer Bones spent learning how to read and write the alphabet, and how to read simple books made up mostly of two-syllable words. She knew that learning how to read the words on the map, instead of just learning the shapes of the states, could only help her with her plan.

Chapter Three

Bones figured that when the Lord was passing out kindness in the Brewster family, he used it all up on Master and his two daughters, because he sure didn't have any left for Master's wife, Old Mistress Polly.

"Musta been a terrible day the day she was born," Granny always sputtered, slowly shaking her head back and forth. "Musta been a dark storm or somethin'." Granny was wiry and thin from working the fields, her hair pure white, and Mama often wondered aloud if the Brewsters were ever going to bring Granny in to work in the big house. Bones worried that they were just going to keep her working in the fields till she dropped dead one day over a tobacco plant.

Old Mistress Polly's disposition was as sour as a briny pickle. While her husband was tall and graceful, she was small and plump, with narrow, gray-green eyes that rested inside little slits under her short forehead.

Sometimes the house slaves would look up to see

her shadowy figure on the wall. They knew she was lurking around the corner, waiting to catch them not doing their chores so she could lurch out with her hickory stick and smack their hands. Many of them took to calling her Wolf Woman behind her back because of her slanty, gray-eyed stare, and everyone tried to stay out of her way to avoid her fits of ill humor. The Brewster sisters never talked back to their mother, and like everyone else, they preferred the company of their father.

It was a quiet autumn afternoon, and a river breeze pushed through the shutters' open latticework. Liza and Bones were excited. The newest edition of *Merry's Museum Magazine* had arrived that morning. Liza had explained to Bones that it was the most popular magazine among children everywhere. It was filled with stories for children about people having daring adventures. Liza's favorite section every month was the puzzles and letters from children to Uncle Merry, but Bones was mesmerized by the stories about foreign lands and the exotic animals that lived there.

"Finish writing the sentences I've given you, and you may look through my new *Merry's*," Liza instructed Bones.

Bones flew through her assigned work, wondering

all the while to herself: *What magic is in this month's magazine?*

She wasn't disappointed. There was a black-and-white engraving of waterfalls in New York, and one of a Christmas tree with little white children dressed in fancy clothes sitting under its branches hung with glowing candles, candies, and small toys.

Bones's heart nearly pounded through her chest when she turned a page and read a title: "Africa: Dr. Livingstone's Journeys and Researches in South Africa." An illustration on the opposite page showed a canoe with seven or eight men being thrown into the dangerous waters, their arms flailing as a monster beast rose from the water. The words beneath the picture read: *Boat capsized by a hippopotamus robbed of her young.*

"Miss Liza? What is this word?" Bones pointed at *capsized*.

"'Capsized,' Bones. It means to overturn in the water."

"Oh my," Bones whispered.

It got better. The next story she found was titled "Africa and Its Wonders."

Lord, if she could only show this to Granny.

"'The trees which adorn the banks of the Zonga are

magnificent,'" she read, hesitating to sound out the last word. "Miss Liza, Africa—she's a powerful, beautiful place," Bones finally announced.

Liza laughed. "Yes, I suppose it is." She suddenly tilted her head toward the bedroom door when she heard the hall floor creak.

Bones quickly put aside her writing paper when she heard familiar steps stealing down the hallway outside Liza's bedroom. By the time the door thrust open and Old Mistress Polly burst into the room, Bones had already picked up her fan and was busy shooing flies away from Liza's face.

Old Mistress's left eyebrow flew up. "How is the reading coming along?"

"Very well," Liza replied. But worry lines pinched her forehead, and she fiddled over her book as her mother's glare bored through her.

Old Mistress's eyes swept the room, landing on Bones's writing pad. When she walked over and picked it up, Bones broke out in a sweat, and her fan began to shake.

"What is this?" Old Mistress asked, her breath warm on the back of Bones's neck.

Before she could answer, Liza spoke up. "Some old papers of mine."

The Wolf Woman squinted harder at Bones's child-like letters, so different from Liza's more graceful, swooping words and curly letters.

Bones looked down and saw her spelling book and the map on which she had printed the states and each state's capital poking out from under her skirt. Mistress suddenly yanked the little black girl up by her arm and snatched the papers from beneath her. Bones's beginning letters were carefully scrawled on page after page next to Liza's.

She did not fully understand why, but she knew in that moment that she was in fearsome trouble. She picked up her fan again and began furiously waving it next to Liza. In mid-swoop, Mistress ripped it away and began swatting her on the head with it.

"Mama!" Liza protested.

"Are you teaching this Negra to read and write?" She turned her crimson-faced anger on her own daughter. "Answer me!"

"I am practicing to become a teacher." Liza stood up as tall as she could and faced her mother square on.

With one quick swipe, Old Mistress Polly struck her own daughter in the face with the fan.

"You do *not* teach Negras to read or to write! It gives them a bad attitude and makes them dangerous,

Liza!" Old Mistress Polly wailed. "And it is against the law."

Sweat dampened her dress under her arms, and her veins pulsed against her temples. Leaning down close to Bones's face, she delivered a good hard slap to be sure Bones was paying attention.

"If I ever find you touching one of these letter blocks or near a book again, I'll have you sold to another plantation, and you'll never see your mother or granny again. You hear me, gal? We sold your father, and we'll sell you, too. You are a slave. Do you know what that means, Bones? You are our property. We own you. You belong to us just like our cows and our chickens and our horses and our tobacco fields. And if we are not happy with those things, we get rid of them. And if we are not happy with you, we will get rid of you. Do you understand what I am saying?" Old Mistress's face was the color of a plum, and her hands were trembling when she finished.

Bones nodded furiously, her hands in tight fists by her sides.

"You're lucky I don't have you skinned. Go back to your cabin. Now!" Old Mistress ordered. "Someone will be there shortly to give you a whippin'."

Bones's feet would not move.

"Run, you little black beast!" Old Mistress snapped. Her hand came down with a slap on the back of Bones's head as the girl finally flew out the door and down the back steps.

Chapter Four

Bones went back to her cabin to wait. No one was back from the fields yet. She quickly took Lovely from around her neck. She dropped her carved peach-pit heart into the wide-mouthed bottle that she used to store it in and hid both the treasures under the sleeping pallet to protect them. She had seen Ben, the hulking black overseer, flog grown men and women, but she had never seen a child whipped. Ben lived alone in a cabin on the other side of the plantation. The Brewsters didn't want him living near them, and it would have been too dangerous for him to live among the slaves' quarters. The other slaves hated him. He showed no hesitation to use his whip on his own people when ordered to. It was not unusual, after a visit from Ben, for a slave to find his kettle or blanket missing. Fortunately, Master Brewster only used beatings as a last resort, so they were delivered few and far between.

Bones heard the sound of Ben's boots dragging in

the dust. He stopped in front of her cabin, and Bones dropped to her knees, her heart pounding in her ears.

Ben stood just outside the closed door, slowly slapping what Bones imagined was his whip against the side of his leg. She smelled cigar smoke drifting through the walls, and the smell turned her stomach. She heard him sniff and clear the phlegm from his throat. He spit into the dirt next to the cabin.

When the door flew open, Bones saw that Ben carried a bunch of hickory sprouts tied together instead of the big leather strap he used on the grown-ups. He also held a bucket that reeked of vinegar.

Her heart fired inside her chest, and she stared at the floor. The air was so quiet she could almost hear his gaze slowly travel around the cabin, looking for some little trinket he might want. Her eyes squeezed shut, and she listened as his feet shuffled around the room, stopping here and there. He paused in front of the fireplace, cleared the phlegm from his throat again, and spit it into the embers from the morning's fire, where it sizzled and hissed. He circled her, whistling softly, and then stopped. His eyes slid around, finally settling on Bones trembling on the floor, and he let out a long sigh, as though he was bored by this puny little chore in front of him.

"Pulls your shirt up, gal," he drawled, looming above her. He smelled of sweat, tobacco, and liquor.

"Please," she whimpered, clasping her knees tight.

"I said, pulls your shirt up. Gals that don't hear so good gets it worse," he ordered.

She was afraid she would faint, but she slipped her shirt up to her shoulders. Her ribs protruded like a bird's bones from her narrow back, and her skin felt clammy.

He pulled the handmade whip back and snapped it hard against her back, and she screamed when it bit into her flesh. She hunched her shoulders, and her hands flew up and covered her ears. The hickory sprouts snapped hard across her back again. She shrieked and fell facedown on the floor.

"Oh, pray. Oh, pray." She groaned and tried to crawl under a chair. But Ben grabbed a fistful of her hair and dragged her back.

"Don't try and go nowhere, gal," he growled.

Pulling her knees up underneath her, she tucked her head down when the whip cracked a third time. She bit her tongue, and blood mixed with drool oozed out from the space between her front teeth.

"Oh, please, please, no more, sir," she wailed, words and blood both spitting out of her mouth.

Ben picked up the bucket and snorted. "Gots a little salt and vinegar here for you." He swung the pail back and threw it in her face. "Mistress says to never use them eyes to look at nothin' you not supposed to again."

"I won't, oh no, no, please!" she screamed, shaking her head wildly, and squeezing her burning eyes shut. "Have mercy on me." Bones shuddered.

"Girl," he snickered, "don't expect there's no mercy for you in this world."

With that, he picked up his instruments of torture and calmly walked out of the cabin, Granny's pipe tucked in his side pocket. He left his victim alone in a little wet heap on the floor. For weeks after, the smell of cigar smoke made Bones gag.

～～～～～～～～

The angry purple welts across her back and red, swollen eyes lasted for two weeks. Bones swept and washed the kitchen and porch floors and performed her duties anyway. Mama and Granny were as angry as wet bees with Old Mistress Polly, but knew to keep their fury to themselves. They applied cool homemade salves to Bones's back and face every morning.

Lying in her bed at night, Bones went over and

over the map in her mind, being certain not to forget any details. When she found out what state her pappy had been sold to, she would know how to get there—which direction to go. In the darkness, she traced each letter of the alphabet on the inside of her arm with her finger, imagining each state and its place on the map.

V-I-R-G-I-N-I-A.

South of Virginia, shaped like one of the boots that Master wore when he rode his horses: L-O-U-I-S-I-A-N-A.

South Carolina—shaped like a wedge of Queenie's shoofly pie. *They cannot beat the learnin' out of me*, Bones thought defiantly. *South Carolina, Georgia, Florida . . .*

"She get hers," Granny would fume about Old Mistress. "God seen it all and marked it down. She nothin' but an old, rich devil."

At first, Bones was certain that Liza would come find her, but as the days went on, the truth in Mistress's words settled on her. They were not friends. The Brewsters owned her. In Bones's heart, though, she still believed there was something more than that between her and Liza.

During those two weeks, she slept naked on her

stomach until her wounds closed up. The stinging cuts were eventually replaced with three jagged scars shaped like lightning strikes that ran across her back.

Chapter Five

The wind seeped through the gaps in the cabin walls all through the night, reminding the women that cold weather was coming. They would patch them up with mud before the air got colder. Master would appear one day soon with shoes for all his slaves, as he did every year. They felt lucky in this way. Many plantation owners let their slaves go barefoot all year. Frostbite was common.

The sound of the wind made it hard for Bones to sleep, and Granny's nose made a whistling sound when she snored. The old woman and the wind took turns. The wind would rise up and heave through the old cabin. Just when it would stop, Granny's nose would start up again and let go a long snorty whistle. This went on most of the night. The wind, Granny's nose, the wind, Granny's nose.

"You need to forgets about that readin', Bones. It can only be trouble for you," Mama said as they lay in the darkness. Bones slept in the middle between her granny and her mother on sacks stuffed with straw. Lovely, wrapped in her handkerchief, slept tucked under her arm.

"I can't, Mama. Once you knows it, it sticks there. I can't help it. And Miss Liza didn't mean to get me in trouble."

"I know that," Mama said. "But you old enough now to know that slaves are sold off for knowin' how to read. Sometimes they even killed. You need to wash that learnin' outta you brain. Please listen to me now."

"Mama?" She hesitated. "Why they sell my pappy?"

Her mother rolled onto her back and rested her face on the edge of the rough sack, pieces of her hair escaping from the bun tied up on top of her head. She had soft, wide brown eyes, but hard work had beaten her face so she looked older than her twenty-seven years. Still, as her mother lay there with a little sliver of moonlight coming through the cabin and resting just so across her face, Bones could imagine what her long-lost pappy must have seen in her. Bones had the same soft round eyes as her mother, but Mama's had grown squinty from working in the sun for so many years.

"The crops was poor that year," Mama finally said. "Didn't need so many men. Masta up and sold him and two more men. Just took him one mornin', and I ain't never seen him again. Mm-hmm. He was a handsome man, he was—tall and broad shouldered."

"Why they call him Fortune?" Bones asked. "That's a funny name."

"They called him Fortune because he was good with wood making, and they could sell the chests and bureaus he made for a lot of money," Mama said. "Twice a year Masta Brewster took his chests down to Richmond. Anyway, he was stubborn like a mule. Didn't want to belong to no man and kept trying to run off. They would have killed him or chopped off his hand, except then he wouldn't have been able to make furniture for them no more. So they took an ax and chopped off his left ear instead. That stopped him runnin'," Mama said.

"He didn't run again, Mama?" Bones asked.

"No. He just do what they say and come home every night to me and you and Granny. Then one day they call him and two others up to the big house, and I never see him again. Never even let him say good-bye."

"Tell me again about the day I was born. When Pappy give me his heart." Bones rubbed her little carved heart between her fingers.

"Well," her mama began, sounding too tired to talk. "You come right out, and your pappy say how beautiful you are. He thinks you the most beautiful baby on the whole plantation. And then he pulls a little peach pit out of his pocket that he's carved into the shape of a heart. That man could make anything. And he'd carved tiny vines and a flower all over that heart, and he put it in your little hand."

"And what did I do then, Mama?" Bones asked.

"You closed your tiny fingers around it. We couldn't believe it! And then Fortune say, 'Now my baby girl will always know she gots her pappy's heart in her hand.'"

"I just love that story, Mama." Bones sighed. "Where do you think my pappy is? You ever hear anything—anything at all?"

"No. But somewhere far away. Maybe Mississippi, I hear, or someplace called Alabama." She covered her eyes with her small hands as if to wipe out his memory. "Lord, I loved that man. And they just up and sold him—sold my Fortune," Mama said.

"Just like he was any old thing," Bones said softly.

"You go to sleep now," Mama said. "Roosters be crowin' good mornin' to us before you know it."

"I will, Mama," she whispered, trying to remember how many s's were in Mississippi—the state shaped like a piece of bread with a bite taken out of it.

She pulled her little nightshirt up over her eyes, snuggled Lovely close to her heart, and thought, *Snug in my little cabin, but still with my sorrows, worth no more than a cow, or a horse, or a dog.*

Chapter Six

"Old Mistress wants all the silver polished so you can sees yourself in it," Queenie instructed as she finished mixing up the paste. "I'm gonna be checkin' on you 'cause *she* gonna be checkin' on me!"

Bones wrinkled her nose. "It smells funny," she said.

"That's why you not gonna be polishin' in my kitchen house," Queenie said.

She led Bones outside to the picnic table next to the big house. Queenie often sat there on sweltering days and chopped green beans and carrots, or diced potatoes and onions.

Today she had spread old newspapers on top and had more than two dozen pieces of Old Mistress's silver laid out.

"Get to work, gal," Queenie ordered. "And don't miss any little corners or edges!"

Bones sat down on the bench and began polishing a water pitcher in neat little circles with the creamy white paste. The smooth surfaces were easy. It was the decorative areas—the vines and twining roses—that took the longest. They reminded her of the little leaves and vines her pappy had carved into her peach pit. That made her smile. She dug her fingernail into the little crevices to work out the tarnish. When she finished the pitcher she held it up and looked at her reflection. *Pretty cute*, she thought. She stuck her tongue through the space between her two front teeth. Mama said that when Bones got older that space would close up. Mama said she had that same space when she was a child, and by the time she was grown it was gone. Bones would like it if her ears didn't stick out from her head quite so much, but she figured she was stuck with them for good.

She moved the water pitcher over slightly to one side, exposing the newspaper underneath. She looked around carefully before lowering her eyes to read the paper. There was an article about an upcoming Thanksgiving Ball in Richmond. *Well, well*, Bones thought. Another stated that Mrs. So & So had ladies over for a luncheon. Nothing all that interesting, but it still felt good to be able to read, and to know that the learning had stuck good in her head.

Bones looked down at her hands, white now from the polishing paste, and said out loud, "Well, I declare, I think they look prettier black!"

She was interrupted when the window above where

she was working slid open, and she heard Liza say, "I need you to help me with my sewing, Jane. I can't get the hem on my doll's dress to hang straight."

Bones scanned the yard to be sure there was no one around her, and then she tiptoed over and stood under the open window. She couldn't see the girls but she recognized the next voice as Liza's older sister, Jane.

"Give me your sewing basket and thread your needle. It's just a matter of practice. I'll show you," Jane said. "And I understand you will have plenty of time indoors to practice. Mama says that she is horrified at the direction your character has taken, and you will be spending more time indoors practicing more ladylike pursuits."

"So she says." Liza groaned.

Bones leaned against the house where she could better hear the conversation.

"What could you have been thinking, Liza, teachin' that little Negra gal to read and write?" Jane said.

"I've decided that I am going to be a teacher when I'm grown. I was practicing on Bones. Mama didn't have to have her beaten," Liza said. "It was my idea to teach her. I was watching from my bedroom window when Ben went down to Bones's cabin, and I heard her screams all the way up here. It was so terrible!"

"Regardless," Jane said. "The little blackie needed to learn her place."

"I miss playing with her. You have the Anderson twins," Liza sputtered. "All I have is you!"

"Well!" Jane said, bristling. "I beg your pardon?"

"I mean that you like to just read and sew, and I want to go out and run in the fields and play with the dogs," Liza explained.

"You'll never catch a man if you keep carrying on that way," Jane said. "No one will want a wife who acts like a wild little boy!"

"I don't want to catch a man!" Liza insisted. "I want to be a teacher."

"Oh, Lord, Liza Anne Brewster," Jane said. "You go ahead and teach, then, but I'm going to be the lady of a plantation just like Stillwater someday. You'll be some raggedy poor old teacher—probably a spinster at the rate you're carrying on. But don't worry, you can come visit me, and I'll give you my hand-me-downs."

At least she misses me, too, Bones thought, crouched against the wall in her hiding spot.

Chapter Seven

Most Sundays the slaves were given the afternoon off. One Sunday in late September, Master Brewster pulled up on his black horse hauling a wooden cart. Bones sucked in her breath when she saw Miss Liza was with him, sitting high atop her own horse, her pale blonde hair tied up in pretty braids.

Master rang a big bell that was attached to the wagon, and his voice boomed across the slave yard. "Boots or shoes for everyone!"

Doors opened up and down the long row of cabins, and women came out with babies on their hips, even though there were no shoes for babies. Men who were fishing down at the river put down their poles and came up to stand in line. No one wanted to miss a chance for a pair of shoes.

Bones stood mesmerized in her doorway, Lovely swinging from her neck. She looked up at Miss Liza, her legs swung primly sidesaddle. She hadn't been allowed to play with or even talk to her since they had been caught by Old Mistress with the books. It was odd to see her here in the slave quarters, in the middle of Bones's world.

"Agnes May, are you coming, gal?" Master looked directly at Bones.

She stared blankly back. She turned her head and looked behind her, but there was no one there. Who was he talking to?

"I'm speaking to you. Bones?" he said.

She stepped out and got in line.

What did he call me? she asked herself.

Miss Liza slid delicately off the horse and walked straight up to her. "Agnes May. That's the name you were born with, silly. Bones is your nickname."

Just like that. Not a word to each other in weeks, since she'd had the beating of her life, and up Liza comes, as if nothing but time had come between them. And Bones had never before heard this name —Agnes May.

"You can come up to the house some day after the crops are in, and we'll play with my dolls," Miss Liza said. "Mama says we can. You can bring Lovely, too." She took Bones's hand and placed two little black buttons in her palm. "These are for Lovely. Now she can have some eyes. Just press them onto her face."

Agnes May "Bones" Brewster smiled a little and said, "Thank you, Miss, I'm grateful." Liza smiled a little, too, spun on her dainty slipper, and hopped back up on her horse.

That night, Bones sat next to Granny on the cabin door stoop while Granny puffed away on the new corncob pipe she had made to replace the one Ben had stolen. They liked to sit together in the quiet just before bed to relax and watch the stars flitter in the sky.

Granny had pulled off her shoes and dusted fresh herbs in them. Bones thought she always walked as though she had a stone in her shoe, but Granny said it was rheumatism that made her limp. Every week she placed fresh sprinkles of red pepper in her shoes, and on nights when her rheumatism really bothered her, she would drink a boiled tea made from the same dark flakes. This was just one of Granny's remedies. She said you could get most everything a body needed from the fields and the woods. But Bones noticed that as she got older, Granny's limp only got worse, especially when the weather was damp.

Crouched in front of the cabin next to theirs was a tall, lanky boy a couple of years older than Bones. He was singing and picking softly on a banjo he'd carved from a gourd. *"Rabbit in the briar patch, squirrel in the tree, wish I could go huntin', but I ain't free."*

"Franklin, how you learned to play and sing so good?" Bones called over.

"My pappy teach me before he sold," he said, smiling sweetly at her.

"You pappy teach you good, Franklin. I don't know if my pappy could play music, but he could sure make furniture that was as beautiful as a song. Mama said he carved birds and flowers and fruit into the wood—fit for a queen!"

"Um-hmm," Granny agreed. "That man could turn an old pine knot into a rose with just a little old jackknife."

Bones opened up her hand and showed Franklin her carved heart.

"What is that?" he asked.

"It's a peach pit! My pappy carved it special for me." Bones smiled. "And it's my pappy's heart that he give to me when I was born."

"Well, now," Franklin said. "You are sure right 'bout that. It is beautiful."

Bones loved this time of day, sitting with Granny. Sometimes the old woman would break her silence, telling stories about their ancestors and tales of Africa. She said her grandpappy had been a king in Africa where their people came from. When she got to puffing away on her pipe, she'd get all wound up and spout out wondrous tales of magical lions or tortoises and the awful tricks they would play on people.

"How old is you, Granny?" Bones sat close to her wiry, little grandmother and picked at some pecans. "You gots a name besides Granny?" She had more important things on her mind tonight than stories of ancestors and talking animals.

"I don't know exactly how old I is, but I knows my name," Granny answered. "It's Lucy. Yes'sa. My mammy and pappy was borned in Africa, that's what they told me. I was born on the Carter Plantation upriver, and when they sold me here, Mistress Carter said to be sure to tell 'em you's borned Lucy Carter. Then they be sure to put you down in their slave book. But when they sell me to the Brewsters, they say they put my name in the book as Lucy Brewster. That because you take the last name of the folks who owns you.

"Lawd, ole Masta Carter, he own so many Negras he didn't know his own slaves when he seen them. He stops them on the road and say, 'Whose Negras are you?' They'd say, 'We's Masta Carter's Negras.'

"He'd say, 'I am Masta Carter.' And he'd drive on." She slapped her leg and laughed. "But Missis Carter was good to us Negras. And they didn't whip us like some owners did. But they done sold us if they don' need us. Your mama and me, we so happy when you become a house Negra—because house Negras get plenty to eat. Like ham and extra corn bread. That's why Queenie so fat! Lord. That woman think the sun come up just to hear her crow."

Granny's nose wrinkled up like she smelled something funny, and she spit a long stream of dark tobacco out the corner of her mouth and off to the side of the cabin. Granny didn't take much liking to Queenie. She said she put on airs because she worked in the big house.

The old woman kept staring up at the sky. "Look like God just took a fistful a stars and throwed them up into heaven," she said.

There was a long pause, and then Bones, her eyes big, whispered, "Did you see it, Granny? Did you see your name in that book?"

The old woman hooted with laughter. "Lawd no! I can't read. But they told me so. All plantations got slave books. That's how they keep track of all the Negras they own and all them that dies."

"You scared of dying, Granny?" Bones asked.

"Oh, no, child. I figured out the secret to bein' happy here on earth, and I figure the Lawd will show me the way when I go home to him."

"What's the secret?" Bones asked.

"Well, nothing would beat being free. That's the

first thing. But whether or not you's free, I figure happiness is three things—someone to love, something to do, and something to look forward to."

"What you got to look forward to, Granny?"

"Why heavens, child! Someday I's going to heaven and there ain't nothin' Old Mistress or anyone else can do to keep me from going."

Chapter Eight

That night, Granny, Mama, and Bones lay together tight as a fist against the early autumn's growing night chill. The field hands would be working seven days a week from now on to bring in the harvest. Bones would be sent to the fields for a while, too. Every man and woman that could be spared was set to splitting and stacking peach-tree wood for the next year. This winter they would use up all the stacks that had been drying since last year. The wood they cut now would dry and be used the following winter. Long, neatly stacked woodpiles were set outside the big house, and a separate one stood behind the slave quarters for their fireplaces. Master Brewster's father had made sure when each cabin was built it had a chimney made of sticks, mud, and stones. When the winter set in, the slaves could have a few pieces of peach wood every day so that even if their cabins were never quite warm, they weren't freezing. Bones knew that you had to plan seasons ahead when you lived off the land.

Wild turkeys had taken to roosting in the trees outside their cabin, and they gobbled themselves to sleep every night. Granny's chest rose and sank silently, too exhausted from the day's work to snore.

"Mama?" Bones whispered. "I named my baby doll Lovely because white folks use that word when they talk about somethin' beautiful." She thought the word left a soft tinkling sound in the air after it left people's lips.

"Why you call me by a funny name like Bones if that's not the name I was born with?" she asked into the darkness.

"Lawd child, why you always set to thinkin' at night when my head is so tired?"

"Why, Mama?" she demanded.

"Old Mistress Polly call you that when she first see you. You was long—skinny legs and arms like a spider. She say you not a nice, fat little baby like her babies. You just all bones. 'That's what we'll call her,' she say, 'Bones,'" Mama explained. "She has the say about names. Used to be a slave named Melissa here for a time. She had a nice little baby boy, and she named him Henry. Old Mistress Polly come to see him soon after he was born, and she laughed and said, 'That little colored baby isn't Henry!' She say his name is going to be Shoofly. Can you imagine that? Old Mistress heard Melissa call her baby Henry once after that, and she slapped her face. Poor little baby was Shoofly after that. You learn quick not to argue with Old Mistress. They sell Shoofly the year after they sold his mama.

"That's why you been Bones ever since. It don't matter what anyone calls you. They just words that disappear in the air soon as they said. They have nothin' to do with who you are. Your mama knows just who you are," she said. A soft smile spread across her face. "Don't ever go against Old Mistress wishes again, Bones."

"I don't like that Old Mistress Polly," Bones whispered.

"I know," Mama whispered back. "But is a dangerous thing not to like her. So don't never say that again."

They had almost drifted off when there was a shuffling noise outside the cabin.

"Mama? You hear that?" Bones asked, sitting up.

"Hush, child. That nothin'," Mama answered. "Lie back down."

But Bones slipped off the bed, sure that she heard Franklin's cabin door creak open.

"Maybe they has to go relieve themselves," Mama whispered.

"I hear voices, Mama. I hear a man's voice." Bones cocked her head and pressed her ear tight to the wall. The only people who lived in that cabin were Franklin, his three little sisters, his mama, Becky, and his granny. No man lived there since they had sold his pappy.

Clutching Lovely in her hand, Bones opened the door just a crack.

"Get back here, you hear me?" her mother snapped. "You gonna rile up the dogs."

She leaped out of bed and went over to kneel next to Bones in the darkness.

"It's Will," Mama whispered, clearly exasperated. "Franklin's pappy. Becky's husband."

"What? But he been sold a few years back." Bones blinked in the darkness.

"I know. He sold couple miles down the river to Colonel Sam Smith, the same Colonel Smith who used to own Queenie. But he sneaks back about every month on a Sunday. They got that day off, just like us. He sneaks up the river to see Becky and their young ones. He waits in the woods. If he hears Franklin playin' the banjo, that means it's safe for him to come that night. If Franklin don't play the banjo, it means it's too dangerous, and he don't come—he go on back to the Smiths'. He be leavin' early in the mornin' afore the turkeys and the roosters wake up."

"What about the dogs? Why don't they bark?" Bones asked.

"He brings two slabs of meat wrapped up in stinkweed that he picks from the riverbank. That way the dogs can't smell it till he gets close. When he unwraps it, they done rather have that meat than chase after Will. And when he leaves in the morning, he unwraps the second piece and the same thing." Mama laughed a little. "If them dogs ever run into Will, Masta be wonderin' why they run up and kiss and love on him like he they long-lost friend. Ha!"

Bones was too astonished to speak.

"You must never ever tell nobody, Bones. They kill Will if they find him. You understand?" There was no mistaking the seriousness in Mama's voice.

Bones thought of the whip and the salt and vinegar and said, "I understand, Mama."

Mama smiled through the darkness. "Can always tell when he come, 'cause he brings her flowers that he picks along the way. Next day, Becky's got them in her water cup."

"Did my pappy ever bring you flowers, Mama?"

The smile slid off Mama's face. "Sometimes. Been so long now I can hardly remember. They sold your pappy so far away he can't bring me nothin' now. Don't have any idea where in God's old world he be. Don't even know if he's still alive."

"I'm fixin' to find him for you when I'm a little older, Mama," Bones confided.

"Don't talk so foolish!" her mother scowled. "That kind of talk will get you in a heap of trouble."

"Well, then, you hafta wait to see him in heaven, Mama," Bones said.

"Maybe so, child, maybe so." They went back to bed.

Bones crept out just before dawn to peek at the cabin next door and secretly watch until Will snuck out into the dim light. Hidden against the back of the cabin, Becky wrapped her arms around him and kissed his face and his neck and his chest. Franklin slipped his long, lanky arms around his father's waist and buried his head in his thick shoulder while his three little sisters clung on Will like newborn puppies. Bones had never witnessed such a complete family wrapped in so much tenderness.

Finally, Will pulled away, unwrapped the meat, and tossed it at the waiting dogs before disappearing into the still dark woods.

~~~~~~~~~~

"My Will says the Northern states gonna fight for sure if the Southern states don't set us Negras free," Becky said the next day. Will had become the slaves' lifeline to the outside world. He was a house slave at the Smiths' plantation, serving in their dining room, which made him privy to dinner conversations. The Smiths entertained a great deal, and talk of trouble with the North was the topic of every dinner conversation with visitors lately. Bones now knew that Will relayed bits of information to his wife whenever he visited her, and she in turn passed it on to the rest of Master Brewster's slaves.

Becky spoke under her breath as she and Mama pulled their hoes up a long garden row. She whispered so Bones, helping in the fields today, wouldn't hear.

"It's all right, Bones saw Will comin' and goin' last night," Mama said.

Becky stopped short and looked fearfully from Bones to Mama.

"Don't worry, Becky," Mama said. "She knows not to tell. She won't tell no one at all. Will you, Bones?"

"I swear." Bones nodded vigorously. "Don't want nothin' to happen to Franklin's pappy like what happened to mine."

But Becky still looked nervous. "You ever say anything, Bones, I swear—"

"I won't!" Bones promised. "I promise! I never say nothin'. Ever."

Becky nodded, but she still glared at Bones as if she would thrash her if she ever broke her promise.

She turned back to Mama and finished her story in a low voice. "Will says settin' slaves free is all folks who come visitin' from the North talk about."

Mama made a face. "No white man I ever know gonna fight for no Negras. Humph."

Bones was silent, but she was taking in every word.

"It's true, Grace. He says it's true," Becky insisted. "They gonna set us free. Only reason we don't hear talk abouts it around here is cause that old Wolf Woman makes sure none of us around when they talkin' about anything. When they serve meals here, they have to scamper right out of the dinin' room. No waitin' around where we might hear somethin' said.

"My Will, he stands around the dinin' table at the Smiths'. He hears all the white folks' dinner talkin'. He says that's all the white folks care about these days. The North stirrin' up talk of a war if the South don't set us Negras free."

"What does that mean? Free. I ain't never been free," Mama hissed. "Don't know what that look like."

"Well, I guess I don't know either. But we's learned a lotta hard things in our life, Grace." She smiled slyly. "So I guess we could learn how to be free."

Chapter Nine

A low rumble of thunder rolled down the river. The air smelled of coming rain.

"Move along," Ben shouted as the last of the slaves dragged themselves up the dusty path from the fields to their cabins. Granny and Mama walked side by side, their hoes slung over their shoulders, their faces seamed with dirt from the fields. Bones lagged behind, swinging the wooden water bucket, still half full so they would have water that night.

House slaves in black jackets were taking in the glass lanterns from the porch tables so they wouldn't blow over if the wind kicked up. Off to the side of the house, a washerwoman took down the last of the dry sheets from the lines, snapping each one in the air before folding it into her basket.

Mama spied Old Mistress Polly first, and her eyes narrowed. Old Mistress was hurrying down the tree-lined path toward the big house with Queenie by her side, issuing orders while waving her hands in the air.

They were coming from the direction of the smokehouse, where several months' worth of salted pork, beef cuts, and ham hung from the ceiling beams. Bones figured she must have been giving the cook instructions about the coming week's meals. It was the first time Mama had seen Old Mistress since she had ordered Ben to beat Bones. The hair stood up on Bones's neck. *Please Mama*, she thought. *Just keep moving and don't look at her, or it'll be nothin' but trouble.*

All the slaves knew better than to look Old Mistress in the eye. Heads bent, they stared down at the ground and straggled along in silence. Bones peeked at her out of the corner of her eye, but then quickly stared down at the ground in front of her. Just ahead she saw Mama's head turn toward Old Mistress. *Don't look, Mama.* Bones wanted to scream. *Don't look at her!*

"And a nice ham for Sunday dinner. Do you have all that?" Old Mistress asked.

"Yes'm," Queenie replied, wagging her head.

Old Mistress seemed to notice the slow-moving group for the first time. She stopped short when she recognized Mama, and her wolf-gray eyes suddenly focused carefully on the other woman's face. Mama, expressionless, bent her head back down and stared straight at the ground. Bones could feel her heart beating through her shirt. Wolf Woman was intent on trying to read if there was any sign of danger lurking in Mama's face, and she leaned forward a bit too carelessly. The toe of her leather-buttoned boot turned under and caught the hoop of her skirt. She did a little hop to try to save herself, to no avail. Her arms swooped about like a bird. She fell forward, caught herself, rocked backward, and spun around once before she finally fell. Her petticoats flew up over her head, and she landed on her elbows.

"Oh missus, oh my Lawd!" Queenie bent down and tried to scoop her up. Ben rushed over and helped. But even before she righted herself, Old Mistress's head spun around and caught Mama's eye as the slightest smile quickly vanished—undetected—from the slave's lips.

Ben and Queenie made a mighty fuss over their mistress, brushing her off and escorting her back into the house. But Old Mistress didn't say a word, and never took her eyes off Mama, following her with a squinty gaze until Mama disappeared into the slave quarters.

Once inside their cabin, Bones, still shaking, threw herself against the cabin door while Granny turned to Mama. She wagged her head and hissed, "Lucky she didn't sees you grinnin', or you'd be sleepin' in the boneyard tonight!"

Chapter Ten

"I can't spare any men to cart off your chairs, Polly," Master Brewster said as he tossed his breakfast napkin on the table. "You know that we need every hand we have to bring in the crops and chop wood this time of year."

Bones rushed to quietly sweep the crumbs that fell from his napkin onto the rug.

"Jack," Old Mistress fussed to her husband. "Nellie Hale said if we drop the two chairs off at her house she would have her shop fix them. The rungs are snapped out, and the seats are about to give way. We have Thanksgiving dinner coming up, and I don't want any of our guests to crash to the dining room floor because we don't have our chairs in proper condition."

Bones kept quiet, but she could see someone was going to have to take the chairs to the Hales' or there would be no peace at Stillwater.

"Have Mabel go, then—she knows the way," Master Brewster said. "I cannot spare one man."

"I suppose I could do that. She can wash the windows another day," Mistress said. She turned suddenly and looked down at Bones before swatting her on the back of the head.

"Lord, stop that wiggling, child!" Bones wasn't sure if she should apologize to her mistress or keep still. She decided to keep quiet. The other slaves had taught her that silence was usually best.

"The girl is driving me out of my mind around the house, always wiggling and twisting her feet and hands," Old Mistress carried on. "I tied her to a chair a few times, but it didn't do a lick of good." Mistress smiled at the thought. "Have Mabel take Bones with her to help, and get the child out of my house for a few hours. And Jack, please make sure you write passes for both Mabel and Bones before you go out in the fields. With all this fuss up North, more and more Negras are being stopped and checked. Just last week, two of the Johnson slaves were in town without passes and were thrown in jail till Frank Johnson went on down and got them out."

"I know, I know," Master Brewster muttered as he disappeared into his study to write the passes.

~~~~~~~~~

An hour later, Mabel sat up tall on the bench seat of the wagon, the two dining room chairs carefully wrapped in old blankets and resting on straw in the back. Her bony fingers, swollen with rheumatism, had a tight grip on the reins.

"You ever been to the Hale farm?" Mabel asked, trying to make a little conversation with Bones as the wagon bumped along the dirt road.

Bones laughed. "I never been off Stillwater in all my life."

"Most the slaves haven't. Ha." Bones knew Mabel was proud that she had often been sent on errands off the plantation. "It's not a long way," she said. "We'll be there and back again before lunch."

"Is we headed north?" Bones asked.

Mabel glanced at her from the corner of her eye. "Why you want to know such a thing, gal?" Bones just shrugged her shoulders, and they drove the rest of the way without talking. Old Mabel filled the time singing some of her favorite hymns, and Bones chimed in whenever she knew the words.

The Hales' home wasn't nearly as grand as Stillwater, but it sat up high on a hill above the river, with long fields rolling down to the water's edge. Bones counted about half a dozen slaves with their backs bent, working in the fields.

Hound dogs ran out from behind the barn and

jumped up and down around the wagon, howling and barking at the intruders.

"Shoo! Get away from here," Mabel hissed. "Where's Mrs. Hale? Old Mistress Polly *told* her we's comin' sometime soon. I don't like dogs ever since I was bit as a child."

The door swung open and a tall, lean woman with blonde hair tied up in a bun stepped out on the porch. "Well, Mabel. I do declare you have brought the chairs and a little helper," Mrs. Hale said.

"Yes, ma'am. I has the chairs wrapped up safe in the back, and this here is Bones," Mabel said. "And my mistress sent over five jars of peach preserves for you all."

"Well, well, then. Queenie's peach preserves! Doesn't get any finer than that!" Mrs. Hale stepped down from the front stairs and sent the dogs scurrying around to the back side of the house with a sharp command. "Why don't you bring the jars of Queenie's preserves inside, and I'll have my girl Cleo fix you and your girl a glass of lemonade. Then you can be back on your way."

She stopped a moment. "You got your passes?" she asked.

"Yes, ma'am," Mabel answered.

"Good, good. Did anyone stop you on the way over?" Mrs. Hale looked directly at Mabel.

"No. No, I think they used to seeing old Mabel out in the cart," she explained. "And they know I'm doing errands for my mistress."

"I do believe you are right, Mabel. Well, go around the back way to the kitchen and have my girl give you a glass of lemonade to share with this one," she motioned to Bones.

"Noah." She waved at a thin, bent slave standing behind her. "Carry the two chairs down to the shop to be repaired. This little Bones child can help you."

"Yes, ma'am." Bones jumped off the wagon and swung the back open to help with the chairs. If she did just as she was told, she might be able to accompany Mabel on other errands. She had been careful on the way over to commit the route to memory.

Noah picked up one chair, and Bones carefully carried the other as she followed him down the hill to the big barn.

Chapter Eleven

"Why they call you Bones?" Noah asked.

"Well, my name is really Agnes. You may call me that, please. Bones is just my nickel name."

"Ah." He laughed. "Nickname, I think you mean."

The barn was two stories high, with six stalls for the horses along one side. On the opposite wall were laths and sawhorses and neat piles of different-sized wood planks.

"Gots some chairs that need fixin'," Noah said to a tall black man bent over a table with his hammer. Two little boys fussed at his feet, playing with scraps of discarded wood.

"Pappy, can we help with the fixin'?" the younger of the two asked.

The man laughed and shook his head. "Not this year. Some year when you's older, son."

He took the first chair from Bones and the second from Noah, who wiped his forehead with the back of his hand. "Much obliged, Fortune. I don't have the wind that I used to have," Noah said.

Bones's feet suddenly felt stuck to the barn floor as if they were nailed there.

She stared—thunderstruck—until the tall man who Noah had just called Fortune turned his head to look at her, and she saw the long, lumpy scar where his left ear had once been.

"What you lookin' at, girl?" he said, smiling. But Bones couldn't speak.

"Pappy. Pappy, why can't we help?" the youngest boy asked Fortune.

"No. Go out in the fields and take some water to your mama. She be lookin' for you about now," he said. "Shoo. Go on now."

"I'll take them out, Fortune." Noah sighed as he led the two little boys out of the barn.

"Can I do somethin' else for you?" he asked Bones. She still stood there, her mouth open and hands trembling by her sides.

"You are Fortune?" she whispered. She didn't recognize the voice that came out of her mouth, it was so strained and shaky.

"That's what they call me. Why? Who are you?"

She forgot her own name for a moment. Finally she whispered again. "Bones. Agnes May. I am Agnes May Brewster, and I have been lookin' for you."

He fell backwards against the sawhorse and stared back at her.

"Oh, my Lord," he said. She noticed that his one remaining ear stuck off the side of his head, same way hers did.

Feeling a little stronger, she shook her head from side to side and said softly, "That all you got to say, Pappy? I been plannin' and schemin' to find you almost my whole life. Mama and Granny has missed you somethin' awful. And all this time. All this time you was right down the road."

"Bones," he uttered, looking down at his big hands.

"Agnes. Call me Agnes. Why you never come to see us?" she asked.

"I got caught running so many times. I run again, Bones, and—"

"Agnes!" she exclaimed, feeling stronger still.

"Agnes. I run again, and they kill me the next time." He turned his head so she could see more clearly where they had taken an ax to his left ear.

"What about my mama?" Bones asked.

He looked up. "How is she? She have another man?"

"No. Still waiting for you, which is more than I can say for you. You got another woman, I see. You got two children?"

"I gots three children now. Just had another baby last month." He spoke the words so low she wasn't sure she heard them right.

Tears welled up in Bones's eyes and ran down her face. But she didn't make a whimper.

"Don't tell your mama," he said, after a long pause. "Let her think I'm in Alabami or someplace far away."

Bones looked around at the half-finished pieces of furniture. A dresser with intricate carvings of flying birds on the drawers. A mirror at least six feet tall carved with looping ribbons and roses waiting for a second coat of gold leaf. *Sure never seen anything more beautiful*, she thought.

She reached in her pocket and pulled out her carved peach-pit heart and held it out for him to see, staring hopefully up into his face.

"What's that?" he asked. "Whatcha got there?"

She didn't answer.

"Is that a peach pit? Huh. That one looks real fine. Whoever did that is good with a carvin' knife. It's kind of shaped like an apple. Is it supposed to be an apple?"

"It's a heart," she said softly, her bottom lip trembling. "Mama said you made it for me the day I was born."

"I did?" He looked at the carving like he'd never seen it before. "Well, if I did that, I sure did a fine job."

It took everything she had not to throw herself into his arms. But she had already lost so much today. She was afraid that if she let go, she wouldn't be able to stop everything inside of her from just spilling out and even after it was all gone—it wouldn't change a darn thing.

Mabel's voice soared through the silence, calling her name. "Bones! It's time to go. Get on up here now."

Bones's mouth was as dry as a cracker, but she managed to say, "Alls the places in the world I dreamed you'd be, *alls the places*—but I never dreamed you be right down the road."

"I'm sorry, Agnes," he said. "You a beautiful little girl—look just like your mama. I'm just so sorry how it all come about."

She couldn't answer him. After all this time, there was just nothing else she could think to say. So she turned around, left the barn, and crawled into the back of the wagon.

"Sit up here and keeps me company, Bones, if you want." Mabel offered, slurping down the last sip of lemonade.

When Bones didn't respond, she muttered, "Suit yourself."

Bones lay in the back of the wagon, her head

propped up on a small bale facing the Hale farm. She stared as it grew smaller and smaller until it disappeared within the horizon. Usually, her hands or feet twitched or fidgeted, but every bit of her energy was focused on thinking about what she would do now. She was as still as the pieces of straw that she lay on. Did he know that he was only a few miles from Stillwater? Had he known that? If he did, would he have come to them like Franklin's pappy? Did he still love her mother? Had he jumped the broom with this new woman? Had he ever loved Bones—longed for her the way she longed for him?

This was the end of something, she knew, and it made her heart ache. Granny told her that happiness depended on three things: someone to love, something to do, and something to look forward to. Bones had Granny and Mama to love. Every slave had more than enough to do. *I'll have to find something else to look forward to now*, she thought.

The wagon rattled up Stillwater's drive just about noontime, and Mabel dropped Bones off by the backfields.

"Old Mistress say to drop you off when we get back so you can carry water to the field hands." She shook her head. "Can't says you been much company, girl."

~~~~~~~~

"You enjoy your ridin' this morning?" Mama came up beside Bones, her face creased with dirt and sweat and a broad grin spread across her face. "You all right? Look like you saw a ghost instead of enjoying a morning off work."

"I'm fine Mama, just old Mabel's driving was so jerky it make my stomach sick. I'm fine now. I'll get some water when I go to the river and be just fine," Bones said, slinging the empty water jugs over her shoulders and running down to the riverbank.

The cool water filled up the clay vessels that hung at each end of the rawhide string around her neck. She thought about what would happen to her if she fell into the river and let it carry her on downstream. Baltimore, she remembered from the maps she'd studied in Liza's room. She would float right on down the James River to Baltimore and then on out to sea. *Nothing holding me here now*, she thought, *except Mama and Granny.*

That night she dropped her carved heart in its bottle under the bed pallet and crawled on top to think things through. She'd just have to adjust her plans. No need to be figuring out the southern states anymore. But all her learning wouldn't be for nothing.

She had a new destination in mind now. Someday. Maybe she'd go when she was a few years older. She'd start readjusting her plans now.

North.

Someday that's where she'd head. North.

Chapter Twelve

"Finish dustin' everything in the dinin' room and then do the same in Masta's study," Queenie ordered. "But don' go movin' anything from its place, you hear?" She tucked a stray hair under her freshly ironed bandana turban. Bones noticed that while Queenie was always trying to tame her unruly hair, it had a mind of its own. Little pieces sprung out the sides or top of her head no matter how tightly she pulled it into a bun or how much she tried to vanquish them beneath her turban. Now that her hair was turning gray, her efforts seemed even more fruitless.

"I hear," sighed Bones, tucking a few rags, beeswax, and a bottle of linseed oil in the pockets of her apron. "Queenie, how old is you?" she asked suddenly. "And is that the name you borned with?"

"Why, I don' know how old I is. But I knows my mammy was Nellie and my pappy was John, and I was born in the summer. They gives me the name Queenie. I got five sisters and five brothers, but I don't know where any of them is. They got sold off before me. I don't know I been sold till Masta call me to the big house and tell me. I belong to Masta Brewster from then on."

She gave the young girl a gentle push. "Humph. It a funny thing, but the jaws is the only part of the body that likes to work. Better get to you chores or you be sold off 'cause you nothin' but a lazybones. I got my cookin' to do here." Queenie carefully shaved pieces from a block of sugar, placing them into a wooden pestle and grinding the sweet slivers to a fine consistency with her mortar. There would be a tart for dessert tonight—filled with figs glistening under a coating of honey, fresh from the plantation's hives.

"Be extra careful around the glass bowls and dishes," Queenie called out. "You drop and break somethin' and Old Mistress—she'll whip you again." Bones, with Lovely swinging from her neck, let the kitchen-house door flap shut behind her.

She worked quickly, inhaling the faint honey smell of the beeswax as she swirled it in round, shiny circles on the dark wood furniture. She moved each of the tall glass hurricane lamps, dusting and polishing under each as she went along.

After finishing the dining room, she carefully moved

books in the study, dusting each one before putting them back exactly where they came from. She couldn't help it—her eyes read the words on the front of each book. But she was careful not to look as if she was reading them, in case old Wolf Woman was lurking around the corner. She was almost finished when she picked up a small red leather volume to dust it. The title written across the front of the book in large black letters caught her eye.

Slave Birth Records, Brewster Plantation

Bones wasn't sure what the word *records* meant, but her fingers froze around the book. Slave birth. She stood motionless, listening for any sound of the Wolf Woman before slowly turning around. She was alone. She placed the book on the table so if she was caught she could quickly close the cover and act as though she were simply dusting. She couldn't read the first page when she opened the worn leather cover. It was written in the curly letters that Miss Liza had told her were called cursive. Turning the pages, she discovered neatly printed entries for every slave that had been bought or born or died at Stillwater Plantation. A page was allotted to each slave in order to record their name, birth date, if and when they had been sold, and the date of their death.

She closed the book and pretended to dust under the table. Had she heard breathing in the hall outside the room? She turned and looked but saw no one and went back to the little book. Flipping the pages as silently as a thief, she came at last to her name. AGNES MAY BREWSTER. She stared gap-mouthed, tracing the letters with her finger, her name fairly blooming off the page.

Agnes May Brewster
Born: July 1843. Colored slave.

That was all. She closed the book and furiously dusted and waxed around the room a second time, always keeping her ears open. Finally, she picked up the little red book again and quickly found her page. Her fingers trembled as she slowly, quietly, and inch-by-inch tore the page away from the spine, folded it in half, and tucked it deep inside her apron pocket. She placed the book back where it belonged and walked quickly out the back door and down the path to the kitchen house, her heart hammering in her ears.

"You finally done, Bones?" Queenie asked as the

girl neatly replaced the linseed oil and dusting rags in the kitchen's cleaning cupboard.

"Yes'm. I'm goin' home now for a minute before I go back down to the fields. Don' feel so good. Linseed-oil vapors got to my head." She shoved her hands in her pockets so Queenie wouldn't notice them trembling.

She ran back to the cabin and took the bottle that held her carved heart out from under the sleeping pallet. She read the page with her name one more time, then quickly rolled it up, stuffed it inside the bottle alongside the carved heart, and corked it. She took a candle from beside the fireplace, lit it, and held it over the cork, letting the wax drip down and seal the stopper around the bottle's neck. Outside, she looked around to be certain she wasn't being watched and crawled underneath the cabin to hide the bottle next to a rock.

The danger of her impetuous act weighed on her more and more as the day went on. Granny and Mama were still working in the fields when she got back to the cabin that evening.

That night it rained hard, the drops making *ping-ping* sounds as they found their way through a small hole in the roof and hit the metal pot that Granny kept by the door. *Thank goodness I sealed the top of the bottle with wax*, Bones thought. What if the rain started a river of mud that ran under the cabin and flushed the bottle out from behind the rock and into the open where someone might find it in the morning? What if some animals drug it out? Bones lay in her space on the straw pallet between the two older women, her mind racing with unruly thoughts of the punishment that was sure to come if her crime were discovered. And this time she knew she would not be alone in the punishment. It was unbearable to think what Old Mistress would do to Granny and Mama.

"Why you so jittery? You thrashin' so much I can't sleep," Granny complained, punching down the straw under her head into a more comfortable shape.

"I'm not," she protested, faking weariness and squeezing her eyes shut. Where could she move the bottle so it would be safe? She considered the woods. But the forests in these parts were infested with panthers and bears, and she had seen bears walking like a man out of Master's fields, carrying ears of corn in their arms. The only time anyone went into the woods, they were on horseback or armed with axes to chop down trees for firewood. For every spot she thought of, she could imagine the Wolf Woman sneaking up on her like a whisper, discovering her, and the whupping and salty vinegar that would follow. She had been warned, and next time it would be worse. She might even be sold. Taken away from her Mama. She wondered if her pappy knew when they called him and the other men up to the big house that they were going to sell him that day or if he thought it was a day like any other. Did he think he was going up to trim Old Mistress's hedges or paint the front door? Did he wonder when they shackled him to the other two slaves and threw him in the back of the wagon how his wife would feel?

Bones would rather die than be sold. Agnes May would rather die.

Chapter Thirteen

The next morning, Bones awoke to the sound of the turkeys plopping down from the trees. She quickly slid out of bed and out the door, and walked around the cabin. There was no bottle lying on the ground in the open. She blew out a deep breath and went back inside.

"You walkin' in your sleep, Bones?" Mama asked, rubbing her own eyes. "What were you doing?"

Bones let out a quick laugh and lied. "No, I'm not walkin' in my sleep. I just thought I heard Queenie comin' with breakfast."

"I told you the Lawd gave you those big ears so you could hear extra good!" Granny said, gleefully. "Listen now. You hear that? That's Queenie's wagon coming now. Bones heard it before anyone else."

The roosters carefully picked their way across the dirt yard, stopping occasionally to crow and yank an unlucky worm from its hiding spot in the damp ground. Doors creaked up and down the rows of slave quarters as people came out for breakfast, carrying their mussel-shell scoops. Queenie's horse-drawn wagon rattled down the muddy road carrying the big pots filled with corn bread porridge and molasses laced with whatever meat was left over from the Brewsters' dinner the night before. She stood and scooped heaping servings onto each wooden tray, her beefy black arms still coated with a dusting of fine white flour from the biscuits she'd made earlier for Master's breakfast.

A half hour later, the trays were returned to the wagon, and Queenie prepared to drive back to the kitchen. The slaves headed off to the morning's work, and the sun began to rise up over the river.

"Bones, Masta wants you to carry water to the field hands again today," Queenie said. "They be workin' extra to get in the harvest. Need every hand they can get in the field." She stared down at the child, her chin rolls bunching up like an accordion. The cook hoisted her broad hips up onto the wagon's seat with a groan. She practically blotted out the sun as she waved for the little girl to follow her back to the kitchen house to clean the breakfast dishes and start preparing for lunch.

"You can brings that little corncob baby doll with you. Too bad she can't carry water, too." Queenie laughed at her little joke.

Bones nodded, chasing behind the wagon up to the pump house to fetch the water gourds. Just outside the kitchen door, Master's dogs lazed by the back steps, waiting to be called to run with the horses. They ate the same meals as the slaves, only the dogs were served first. Bones wrapped the strap around the back of her neck and the two gourds hung down on either side of her chest. She headed down to the river to begin her water brigade, which would go on all day again today: Fill the gourds, go to the fields. When a man or woman raised their hand, she would rush to give them water. When the gourds were almost empty, she would head back down to the riverbank to refill them.

The safest place to collect water from the James River was a small finger of land dotted with scrub pine and dwarf oak that dangled out into the river just below the fields. Currents swirled in a shallow pool on the inside crook of the finger, so a person could easily catch the water here without slipping into the faster-moving river and risk being carried downstream.

Bones's body was in the fields that day, but her mind was drained of all thoughts save for the bottle hidden under the cabin. There was only one name on that page in the bottle—AGNES MAY BREWSTER. There would be no mistaking who had torn it from its place. And she could not bring herself to destroy it. She was someone. It said so on that paper. She was more than just someone's little old belonging. She would have to get it off the plantation. As she crouched down, filling the gourds with the cool river water, she hatched her plan.

The dinner bell rang that evening, long after the sun had gone down. Some of the men were still straggling back from the fields, their shirts drenched in sweat, as Queenie's wagon rattled up with huge pots of dinner. The smell of salt meat, cabbage, potatoes, and shortbread drifted above her creaky wagon. Pulling her mussel shell out of its place in her cabin, Bones was the first in line.

"Well, well. You must be hungry from runnin' back and forth between the river and the fields. Lots harder than fannin' flies away from Miss Liza," Queenie teased.

Bones ignored her. She ate the scoop of food and returned the wooden tray to the wagon.

"Don' be actin' like you can't hear me. With them big ole flappy ears the Lawd gave you, I knows you hears everything." Queenie clucked her tongue. "Get a good night sleep. Need you to carry water again tomorrow, Bones."

"It's AGNES," the little girl shot back.

"What you say?" Looking down, Queenie laughed at the little girl's fierceness.

"I said, it's Agnes. My name is AGNES!" Bones was practically shouting.

Queenie laughed like this declaration was the funniest thing she had heard all week, rolled her eyes, and sniffed. "Well, yes'm. If that's what you say."

"Agnes May," said Bones hotly under her breath. "I am Agnes May. I am a someone."

Chapter Fourteen

Thankfully the wild turkeys were as tired as everyone else that night, and they stopped gobbling early. Lying between Mama and Granny, Bones listened until she was sure Granny's snoring and Mama's gentle seesaw breathing meant they were fast asleep. She needed to be sure. She had been too nervous to chew her supper well, and now it stuck in her chest like a stone.

She took Lovely, with her black button eyes gleaming, off her neck and left the doll tucked safely between Mama and Granny. She slipped off the sleeping pallet from the end so as not to wake the women, and peered out the door, looking up the row of slaves' quarters. She was grateful tonight that theirs was the last cabin, closest to the fields and the river. The primitive door sagged against the floor when opened wide, so she took care to open it only partially, and she squeezed out the narrow opening. Barefoot, she tiptoed around back and crawled, snakelike, under the cabin. She moved slowly, crouching, with her hands in front of her, feeling along. In the blackness of the night, her fingers finally wrapped around the neck of the bottle. She sucked in her breath.

The moon was growing bigger every night now. Soon it would be a full harvest moon, but tonight it showed only half of itself behind shifting clouds in the inky stillness. She didn't dare run at full speed for fear that she would fall and the bottle would break. With light, sure steps, Bones hurried down the path alongside the now-quiet fields, past a pile of peach-tree wood waiting to be stacked the next day. She hesitated. For an instant, she thought she saw something move by the woodpile, and she strained her eyes. Nothing. She tried to keep her mind off the eerie night noises coming from the forest. A bear would be nothing compared to Old Mistress Polly if she were caught. A lantern glowed on the back porch of the big house like it did every night. It helped to keep prowling animals away. No one in the big house was awake as she slouched along, undetected under the big sky. If someone were restless and awoke and stepped onto the porch and saw her out in the middle of the night, there would be no explaining.

Reaching the edge of the river, Bones crouched

down and crept out onto the same finger of land where she had gathered up water for the field slaves earlier in the day. The moon shot glittery streaks, radiating along the surface of the James River. She remembered the map of Virginia on Liza's wall and imagined the river's cool, deep waters rolling along for miles before emptying into the Chesapeake Bay and then pouring out into the Atlantic Ocean. It seemed to her a fine place to set her name free. She allowed herself a long moment to imagine where it might go. Her name and her heart. If only she could squeeze herself and her Mama and Granny into the bottle—they could all float away. *They can own me and beat me and sell me, but a part of me will forever be free*, she thought, the thrill of the idea racing through her. *I'll live forever knowing that.*

Kneeling low to the water, she carefully tossed the bottle out into the stronger currents where it was immediately picked up. It bobbed for a moment before being swallowed up in the blackness, rushing away under the moon to begin its magical journey.

LADY BESS

Beginning in the Blue Ridge Mountains, the James River flows east past a series of rapids and waterfalls until it passes Virginia's capital, Richmond. If the bottle had entered along that part of the river, it would have been less likely to survive. But the plantations were built farther east, on the Lower James, where the waters were calmer. So the bottle traveled under the moonlight, past tall trees where bald eagles roosted, down the historic waterway—the James was the first American river to be named by the colonists.

Reaching the river's mouth, the bottle passed into

the southern portion of Chesapeake Bay, which had been the gateway for the first black slaves brought from Africa. Bones's great-grandpappy, a king in his African homeland, had arrived here in shackles to be sold in the Baltimore slave yards.

In the chop waters where the Chesapeake weaves into the Atlantic Ocean, the bottle was swallowed up by the Gulf Stream current and sped along the underwater highway across the sea.

Chapter Fifteen
ISLE OF WIGHT, ENGLAND, AUGUST 1855

Thursday afternoons are definitely the best part of my week, Lady Bess Kent thought as she picked her way through the sunflowers, lavender, bluebells, and cowslips trailing along the hillside that led down to the dock. The oldest of the fishing boats moored on the northern tip of the Isle of Wight was the *Land's End*, which belonged to Chap Harris. Short in stature and bow-legged, Chap's dark skin contrasted starkly with his crown of unkempt, silver curls and one crystal-blue eye. The other one had been lost in a fight with a pirate or when Chap was stabbed by a jealous girlfriend or in a hand-to-fin battle with a man-eating sea monster. Bess knew the story changed often, and depended on whether or not Chap had consumed a pint of ale with his lunch at The Song of the Sea Tavern. But what she was most curious to know about were the scars that ran around his neck and circled one wrist. The rough marks were much lighter than his skin, and they puckered where the wounds had obviously been left to heal on their own. She wanted to ask him how they came to be, but he acted as though they didn't exist.

It made him all the more interesting to Lady Bess.

"What does your father the duke think of you keepin' company with an old salt like me?" he had asked her once.

"Chap, he thinks I'm at the library," she'd answered, laughing.

"You shouldn't be telling tall tales to your father," Chap had admonished.

"Oh, I'm not." She had held up a bundle of books neatly tied together. "I go to the library every week. I just haven't mentioned that I stop here on my way home."

The old man's tales of his exploits and foreign travels were spellbinding, and Bess found them far more entertaining than learning needlepoint or how to properly pour tea.

"There is no doubt that I will be an explorer like my father when I grow up," Bess announced confidently on this Thursday. "And there is still a good bit of this earth left to explore. I just hope that people don't get to it all before I'm old enough to discover some places on my own. I'm only twelve years old, so I'm afraid I still have to wait a few more years till I can begin my explorations."

"Ah, yes, that's so," Chap nodded. One of the qualities Bess most appreciated in him was that he took her at her word. "I don't doubt you, but you live in such a grand house. And exploring is a hard life, Bess."

"Hmm." She frowned. "Grand, yes, but not awfully happy, I'm afraid, in the years since my mother passed away."

"I'm sorry for that," he said, then returned to the first subject. "If it's an explorer you're aiming to be when you're grown, I can teach you some things that will be useful. For instance, do you know how to tie a ship's knot?"

"No. I've asked my father to teach me when we've gone sailing, but he said ladies don't need to know such things."

"Well," Chap said as he winked at her, "Lady *explorers* are a whole different matter. There are six ways to tie a proper knot on a boat. I'll teach you the next time you come. I pride myself that there's no man alive who can tie a finer knot than Chap Harris. And another time I'll show you how to navigate by using only the stars above."

"Now that would be extremely useful to me," she said.

"Well," he went on, "there are a lot of things I can teach you in the weeks ahead. At least while I'm still here on the island."

"Oh no. Are you thinking of leaving?" Bess asked.

"No. But I'm not planning on staying either," he said, laughing. "I get up each day and do as my spirit moves me."

"Where were you born, Chap?"

"In America. New York," he answered. "But I never want to go back there."

She wanted to ask him why, but he turned away, clearly signaling he was finished with the conversation.

Bent over his work, Chap filleted the fish he'd caught that morning, tossing them into one of four large red buckets. Bess knew that he toted the fish up the hill to Parkhurst Prison every afternoon and left them in the kitchen where the cook would make a watery stew for the inmates unfortunate enough to find themselves guests of the infamous island prison. Once a month, she saw a large ship arrive at the dock, and a few dozen prisoners, shackled to each other by their wrists and waists, would board. They were shipped to Portsmouth and then to trial in London or thousands of miles away to Australia's penal colony.

She'd heard that no one ever came back. It was rumored that hard labor and disease killed at least half of them.

Finished with filling the buckets, Chap hoisted them off the boat.

"I'll help," Bess said as she picked up the two smaller pails and followed him up the dirt path to the backside of the large, rambling gray prison. The path to the back door was well worn and only about a hundred yards from the dock. There were guards and high wires at the front, but not at the back where the cook and cook's help entered.

"How long have you been doing this, Chap?" Bess asked.

"Too long," he answered.

"Then why don't you go somewhere else?"

"I don't really know," he answered. "I don't have any family. Don't own anything except the boat I live on, and she's in need of some repair. Got nothing holding me anywhere, so I might just as well be here."

He pulled a large key from his belt, slipped it into the rusty hole, and the heavy metal door creaked open. The dark hallway was lit by one flickering gas lantern, and it took a few seconds for their eyes to adjust to the darkness. They winced as a dank, foul stench hit their nostrils.

"Poor souls," Bess whispered, cringing. "Who could have an appetite for food when the smell is so dreadful in here?"

The kitchen was a short walk down a hallway, and they left the buckets and turned to leave. But the sound of soft crying behind another door at the back of the room stopped them, and they each pressed an ear to the door.

"It's the room where they keep the boys who've been newly incarcerated," Chap whispered. "Keep them in quarantine from the rest of the population till the guards know they haven't got anything contagious."

"It's not locked," Bess noted. There was only a small sliding latch on the kitchen side of the door that prevented it from opening.

"No, but they're not going anywhere," Chap said. "Must be some poor young fella cryin' for his mum. Come on, we're not supposed to be pokin' around, and I'm sure I'm not supposed to be bringing you in with me."

He locked the door behind them and reattached the key to his belt.

She picked up her stack of books from his boat and headed back down the lane to Attwood Manor with the sound of the boy's weeping heavy in her heart.

Chapter Sixteen

With her books slung over her back, Bess ran most of the way home. When she walked in the front door she heard Mildred, the downstairs maid, muttering to herself in the duke's study. Bess chuckled. She knew exactly what the maid was fretting about. A monstrous stuffed tiger, a full two meters high, was posed rearing on its hind legs glaring hungrily at everyone who entered the study. The beast had had the nerve to try to eat the Duke of Kent when he was on expedition in India. The duke had been gone for months, riding elephants through swamps and jungles, when one day the creature leaped out from the tall grass and ran straight at him. He had taken aim and killed the lunging cat with one shot. He had the tiger stuffed and shipped back to the Isle of Wight. The poor maids who had to dust the striped coat and polish the sharp teeth and fearsome, yellow marble eyes had nightmares ever afterward. It took every bit of willpower Bess possessed not to sneak up behind

Mildred and let out a loud, howling roar. The last time she had done that, Mrs. Dow, the housekeeper, had sent her to her room with no dessert. Mildred had just recently begun speaking to her again, and Bess didn't want to jeopardize that. Attwood could be a large, lonely house, and she needed all the company she could get. Even from timid Mildred.

"You do know he won't bite you, Mildred," Bess announced pleasantly, plunking her books down on her father's desk. "He's quite dead."

"Oh, yes, my Lady, I know that is so. But at night—in my dreams. That's a different matter."

"Well, I personally intend to go to India one day," Bess announced. "I'd like to see one of these beasts for myself."

Mildred just shook her head. "That's one trip I won't be accompanying you on."

When she heard Lady Elsie's footsteps coming down the back stairs, the maid bent down to look busy with her chores, lest the lady of the house think she was lolling about and punish her yet again.

There was no end to the chores at Attwood Manor. There were two hundred windows to clean and a stone entrance hall hung with dozens of portraits of the Kent ancestors to dust. The rambling old estate was kept warm by twenty fireplaces that needed to be fed nine months of the year to keep out the dampness that rolled off the English Channel. The great estate sprawled across fifty acres and had been in the Kent family since the 1700s. The beautiful island was so desirable a location that England's reigning monarch, Queen Victoria, and her husband, Prince Albert, had recently built the grand Osborne House as a retreat from the city.

Elsie, the Duchess of Kent, cleared her throat just in case her stepdaughter and the maid hadn't noticed her looming in the doorway. She would have been hard to miss. She was nearly six feet tall in her stocking feet, though she was rarely seen shoeless.

Bess and her younger sister, Sarah, were fond of calling her Elsie the Shrew behind her back. She was scrawny as a nail and she claimed that rich sauces and sweets upset her stomach. Under her orders, the menu at Attwood had become bland and boring.

"Father's longhorn cattle enjoy a more tantalizing menu than we're served," Sarah often complained. Their father was away in London on business so often that he barely noticed what was placed in front of him when he did dine at home.

"What books have you chosen from the library this week?" Elsie ran a long finger over the string that tied the books together. "My, my, you are ambitious. Five books this week."

"One is on polar exploration, though I don't intend to go there," Bess explained.

"Hmmm." Elsie purred like a sly cat. "Too chilly."

"And another one is about New Guinea. That looks like it would be a paradise if you could avoid the man-eating tribes. The one I'm most anxious to start is about the River Nile in Africa."

"Oh, your father and his constant going on about that Nile River!" Elsie rolled her eyes.

"He has the heart of an explorer," Bess defended. "As do I!"

Bess held up a magazine, saying, "And this is my favorite of all. Last month's issue of *Merry's Museum Magazine*. If you want to learn about the Nile River . . ."

"I do not." Elsie sniffed.

"Well, if you wish to learn about almost anything in the world," Bess countered, "it will eventually be written up and explained in *Merry's Museum Magazine*."

Elsie squinted at the cover. "Is that an old man sitting on a stool?"

"Yes," Bess said. "Poor Uncle Merry is in bad health due to rheumatism. But he has traveled the entire world, and every month he shares his stories with children. There are puzzles and songs and pictures and poems, as well. It is all very useful to someone like me who intends to explore the world when I'm old enough."

"Yes, yes, lovely. Well, I might suggest on your next visit to the library you choose a book on keeping house or gardening. Something a lady might be interested in. Goodness, Bess, look at yourself. Your hair is a mess."

"I've just run all the way home from the library," Bess explained, trying to pat down her long black hair.

"Hmmm," the duchess murmured. "Your hair always seems to be a mess and you cannot sew or cook and in the garden—well, I'm afraid you don't know a tea rose from a dandelion."

She picked up Bess's hands in her own and said, "Nails nibbled down to stubby little nubs. Tsk, tsk. You need to start acting and grooming like a lady. You are twelve years old."

"I'm sorry, but I seem to bite them when I'm excited, and there just seems to be so much to be excited about in the world. Honestly, I don't understand how some girls accomplish it. Getting all prettied up. And to be perfectly truthful, it just doesn't interest me at all. I find it all to be deadly boring."

"You need to develop an interest in it, Bess." Her stepmother's brow arched, and she waved a hand at Mildred, who was madly dusting and waxing in front of the drapes. "It's unacceptable when the maid looks more polished than a lady in the house."

Bess cringed, unable to bring herself to look at Mildred. Now she just wanted the conversation to be over quickly before Elsie inflicted any more verbal damage on the poor maid. She nodded. "I will begin putting my best foot forward."

"Well, I do hope you will try." The duchess shook her head slowly back and forth to show her weariness with it all. "Dinner will be ready in an hour, so I'll see you then. And Mildred?"

Elsie pulled aside one of the heavy damask drapes. "Don't forget to dust *behind* the drapes as well as in front, will you?"

"Yes, Your Grace," Mildred replied, although the duchess was already halfway out the door.

Chapter Seventeen

The day after her weekly visit to Chap's boat, Bess and Sarah finished their lessons with their tutors early. Bess asked Gertrude, the cook, to pack them up a small bag with biscuits and a container of sweet, milky tea so that they could have a snack when they reached Singing Beach. Mrs. Dow looked over the snack and made sure to put extra cookies in the bag.

"Remember to be especially careful around the cliffs," she instructed. Ida Dow had been hired by their late mother to be Attwood's housekeeper, but she had turned out to be much more. With her kind heart and unrelenting tolerance of Elsie, she had become the closest person to the girls since they lost their mother.

After a light lunch in the kitchen, Bess and Sarah set out with their dog, Sunny Girl, leading the way.

With the stone house behind them, the sisters walked through the rolling fields, past the apple orchards laden with fruit, and along the narrow paths that led down the cliffs to the ocean. Grapevines plump with fruit tangled through the bushes and stone walls, and birds swarmed them hungrily. Their father taught the girls that ripe grapes were a sure sign that summer was ending.

In less than ten minutes the smell of salty ocean air got stronger, and they could hear a squadron of gulls signaling to each other above the waves.

Cliffs rose up on either side of the narrow beach and sheltered a small cove. Ever since they were small, Bess and Sarah had been warned not to climb the cliffs or play at the foot of the rocky jetties. The English Channel's currents sometimes sent in rogue waves that could carry unsuspecting beachcombers out to sea. Resting the picnic basket down next to a rock, the girls set out to hunt for unusual shells.

"Don't put them in your skirt, Sarah," Bess ordered. "The maids will never get the smell out. Use the bag that Gertrude gave you."

Hunched over their work, they combed through seaweed and broken shells and were occasionally rewarded with a delicately sculpted winkle or whelk. They had to keep a constant eye on Sunny Girl, because she was more interested in the snack bag and the biscuits it contained than sea glass, driftwood, and shiny limpet shells.

"Sunny Girl!" Bess called out. "Come. Come here!" She whistled her best low whistle that her father had taught her, and the dog turned and bounded back across the sand.

But she stopped short before reaching the girls and began digging at something shiny poking out of the sand.

"What is it now?" Annoyed, Bess rushed up to where the dog was pawing, certain that it would be some dead, smelly animal.

Sticking up from the sand was the top of a half-buried bottle. After ordering the dog back, Bess grasped the sand-pitted object by its neck and gently rocked it out of the damp sand. It was scratched, and the stopper was sealed tightly with wax. A rolled paper was clearly visible inside.

"Pirates!" Sarah cried, coming up from behind Bess.

"There are no pirates around here. For heaven's sakes, Sarah. Well, I don't think there are." Bess held up the bottle and twisted it around and around, carefully examining it. The sisters looked at each other and Sarah said, "The Russians?"

"We've been at war in Crimea for a while now, but I don't believe that Russian soldiers are tossing bottles with notes in them out onto the sea," Bess said.

They carried their potential treasure up to the dry rock where their picnic awaited before scratching away the wax with the sharp edge of a mussel shell and gently prying out the cork. It popped out with a *swoosh*.

Bess plucked out the rolled-up paper with her fingertips. She unfurled it and slowly read aloud:

Agnes May Brewster
Born: July 1843. Colored slave.

She turned the bottle around, inspecting it from all angles.

"What does it mean?" Sarah asked. "Is it some kind of sign or omen?"

"Don't be superstitious," Bess ordered. She shook the bottle upside down, and a small carved heart tumbled out. She picked it up from the palm of her hand to closer inspect the tiny carved vines and little flower buds that wound around it.

"It's clearly been carved to be heart shaped," Bess said. "Although I'm not sure from what."

"Really, we were meant to find this," said Sarah. "I'm sure of it. It might be a sign. Or a message. Maybe from Mummy!" Her eyes widened at the thought of it. "That could be it. It could be from Mummy, couldn't it?"

"I don't think so, Sarah. Mummy is with the angels now."

"Bess! How do you know that the angels aren't over the sea?" Sarah asked.

"She's my age," Bess noted as she read the paper over again. "Born July 1843. Agnes May Brewster."

"Do you think this is really from some colored slave?" Sarah mused. "Maybe she was lost at sea on a raft, surrounded by hungry sharks, and with her last bit of strength she tossed this bottle overboard with a note and the heart trinket, hoping to be rescued."

"It's possible. I don't know, Sarah, I don't know. We need to think about it, though. We can't trust anyone with this. You cannot tell anyone, do you understand?"

"Yes, yes, of course," Sarah agreed. "Maybe it is some sort of plea for help?"

"No. It doesn't indicate anything of the sort. Of course, the good news here is that it doesn't appear to be from the Russians," Bess noted.

"Oh, Bess," Sarah said hopefully. "I still think it could have something to do with Mummy."

"Sarah, I wish that were so," Bess said softly. "But I don't believe that."

Both girls took their time as they smoothed the

rumpled note, touching the simple printed words and envisioning different possible explanations.

"Just think, Sarah. Imagine the adventures this little vessel has experienced. I almost wish I could stuff myself inside and be tossed back out to experience the world!"

After a while, they knew Mrs. Dow would miss them at home.

"We can't take it back with us, Sarah," Bess said.

"Snoopy Elsie will find it," she agreed.

"Maybe. But even if I could get it back to the house and hide it, I'm afraid someone will see us coming back with it."

"We could hide it in the bag," Sarah suggested.

"Oh, and I suppose you think that Gertrude or Mildred would keep it a secret if they should find it? I hardly think so. Then I'd have to worry about getting it back out again undetected. It's just safer to hide it here, away from Attwood. I'll come back on my way to the library on Thursday and take it to show Chap. He'll have a good idea where it's from."

"You think you can trust him?" Sarah asked.

"More than any adult I know, except Papa and Mrs. Dow," Bess answered.

They pulled a few small rocks out of the headwall

to create a little cave, above the high-tide mark where their newfound treasure would be safe from the rains, tides, and animals. They could come back again and safely examine it, but for now they needed to return home. They poured the tea out onto the ground, fed the biscuits to Sunny Girl, and hurried back across the fields and paths to the great stone house.

Chapter Eighteen

"I'd rather pretend we're going to a fancy ball," complained Sarah. Bess diligently wove chamomile flowers into her sister's long dark braid before tying a handkerchief like a band around her own head.

"Any fool can get themselves off to a ball, Sarah," Bess explained. "We are preparing ourselves for the true adventures that are going on in the world this very minute. We don't know that Agnes May Brewster tossed that bottle overboard before she drowned. Perhaps she is living right now on a plantation in America as someone's slave. There are all sorts of incredible things going on all over the world.

"But for today's game, I have read about the native people called Indians living in the American West. They are a thieving, bloodthirsty group that paint their faces and go around practically naked, murdering the settlers."

"The Indians are the natives?" Sarah asked, her brown eyes flickering.

"Yes, that's what I've read," Bess confirmed.

"Perhaps they aren't happy with people coming and taking over their country, then. Maybe that's why they are murdering and thieving. How would you like it if people landed their boats on the Isle of Wight and started taking everything over?"

"Well, I don't know the whole story," Bess answered. "And I don't think I will until I am old enough to visit America and get the straight truth for myself. But until that day, we need to practice our skills. Here, put this around your shoulders and pretend it's a sacred Indian blanket."

Sarah stood draped in an old, frayed bed cover from their dress-up chest, her hair laced in white flowers with a feather sticking out of the top, reluctantly waiting for her orders. "Tomorrow can we play fancy ball?"

"Yes, yes, you goose," Bess said.

"You're not just saying that?" Sarah asked. "Last week we pretended every day that we were British soldiers fighting the Russians. Before that we explored India like Papa at least a hundred times. If I fight off a pretend tiger one more time I shall save it the trouble and kill myself! This week it is Indians every day, and now I can see slavery in my future. I'm tired of all this violence. I want to play fancy ball. Do you promise?"

"Yes, I promise," Bess said. "And may I remind you that we are still at war with the Russians in Crimea. You'll be glad some day that you were prepared, should the Russians defeat our boys and decide to land on our little island next."

"Could such a thing happen?" Sarah asked.

"Who knows in this world." Bess tucked a pretend knife in her belt and slung a branch shaped like a rifle over her shoulder. "I'll put my head down now and count to ninety-nine. You go off somewhere and hide. Don't make it too easy. I'm the scout, and I'm going to track you down."

Sarah's eyes narrowed. "And then what will you do to me when you find me?"

Bess remembered when she'd tackled her sister last week when Bess had been a British soldier and Sarah had been the Russian enemy soldier. Sarah had flopped facedown on the grass, and Bess felt bad that she still had scabs on her knees.

But the game must carry on anyway. Bess cocked one eyebrow and gave Sarah a wicked glance. "I suggest, my pretty, that you don't get caught." Bess buried her head in her knees and began. "One, two, three . . . Go boldly, Sarah!" She snickered. "Four, five . . ." Listening carefully while she counted, she made note of which direction her prey ran. "Ninety-eight, ninety-nine."

Straightening up, Bess took in her surroundings with confidence. She had twisted her long black hair up into a bun and fastened it with barrettes to keep it out of her way. They had left Sunny Girl in the house. It would be too easy to find one another with the dog's keen nose. That would have taken all the sport out of it.

The field, dotted with ancient apple trees and tall, dark-green yews, stretched out nearly flat in every direction. Sarah had taken off running to the east, but Bess was too clever to be fooled by this ruse. Chap had told her that when giving chase, expect your prey will try to throw you off by first heading in one direction only to change course when they are out of sight or earshot. Bess learned a great deal from her seafaring friend, which she, in turn, had taught Sarah. She figured that her sister would have run for no more than a minute in one direction, and then turned and gone a different way. Leading with her branch-rifle, she walked purposefully toward the west. It wasn't long before she spotted a freshly twisted chamomile flower on the ground. She smiled to herself.

She would march on to the edge of the field and scout the perimeter, searching for more evidence of where her prey might have entered the woods. She had barely reached the edge of the field when she heard the sound of her sister's bloodcurdling scream. She spun around and looked out toward a lone apple tree twenty yards ahead, where she saw Sarah waving her arms high up in the tree. Sarah crashed down through the lower branches and landed with a thud on the ground below. She jumped up, still screaming, and began to run. A dark wave of angry wasps surrounded her and dived at her head—each blistering sting provoking another howl. Bess ran toward her sister, and by the time they reached each other, the winged tormenters had turned and retreated back to their hive in the apple tree.

Red welts had already begun to spring up on Sarah's face and hands, and her hysterical crying filled the field and carried toward the house.

Gertrude and Mrs. Dow, skirts flying, dashed out the kitchen door. Gertrude was wielding a rolling pin like a weapon above her head. The stable master, who had been down grooming the horses, dropped his brushes and came running, too.

When everyone reached Sarah, her eyes were wild and rolling, and she was gasping between sobs. She looked up at her sister, pulled the feather from her headband, and threw it at Bess. "See what you've done! Stupid Indians!"

All eyes turned toward Bess, and her face flushed. "I didn't tell her to go up into a tree with a wasp nest," she said.

"I do regret your experience," she went on. "But you have clearly survived and will perhaps be a stronger woman for it."

There was a collective groan from the adults as they hustled the whimpering Sarah off to the kitchen to be treated with salves and cold wet cloths.

Once Sarah's stings were tended to, Gertrude poured cups of tea for all of them.

"I'm sorry. I truly am." Bess felt worse as her sister's face continued to swell.

"We know that, my dear," Mrs. Dow said in a calm voice. "But you need to be more careful on your adventures, especially when you have your younger sister with you. I needn't remind you of the frightful spill you both took when you were out lumbering around on those wooden stilts."

"Rest assured that in the future, I will indeed be more cautious. I'm sorry for all . . . ," Bess said as she waved her hands over her sister's head, ". . . all this."

"I forgive you," Sarah said with a gallant smile.

"There, now," Mrs. Dow said to Bess. "You have apologized, which is good for your soul, and Sarah has accepted your apology, which is good for hers. The matter is closed."

Chapter Nineteen

Elsie tapped her nail on her list of things to do that day.

"Mrs. Dow, please take the girls into town this morning. Have them fitted for and order new shoes for both of them. New boots for winter, too."

Bess scowled. She was anxious to check on the bottle and take it to Chap to examine. "I was thinking of going to the library," she said. "I have some books that—"

"Well, you can do that another day," Elsie snapped. "Besides, every time you come back from the library you smell like an old fish! What in heaven's name are you doing at that library?"

"After I get my books, I walk home along the beaches," Bess replied.

"I suggest," Elsie said, scowling, "that you stick to the paths and the lanes, then."

Within the hour, Eldridge, the driver, pulled the carriage up and helped the two girls in before holding his arm out for Mrs. Dow.

"It's a pleasant day for a ride." Mrs. Dow leaned forward. "Let's go the back way so we pass the Queen's property. It's so lovely at this time of year."

Only a few miles of narrow lanes and curving bays separated Attwood from Osborne House, where Queen Victoria and Prince Albert summered with their eight children.

They passed by the pastures that held the Queen's grazing sheep, gravel crunching under the carriage wheels. Stone walls crisscrossed the estate, and at one crossroads, four men were busy repairing a section of wall that had toppled over. Eldridge tipped his hat to the workers, who looked up and waved. Three of the workers were older, but one was a dark-haired boy who looked to be around Bess's age, and she nodded politely when she realized he was staring at her.

"Put your back into it now, Harry," one of the older men admonished the younger one. The boy called Harry snapped to attention and bent down, but not before smiling broadly and tipping his hat to Bess.

～～～～～～

After they finished their errands in the village, Bess was quiet on the carriage ride home. As they rounded a curve near the crossroads, she kept an eye out for the group of stonemasons repairing the Queen's wall. Just as the carriage pulled around the bend, one of the men brought his sledgehammer down to split a boulder. The sharp, loud strike startled the horses, and despite Eldridge's best efforts, they bucked, flipping the carriage and tossing all the passengers onto the road.

Eldridge jumped up from the ground, and along with the stoneworkers, rushed over to help Mrs. Dow and the girls. The boy, Harry, rushed to the side of the frightened horses, grabbed the harnesses, and calmed them with a soothing voice.

"Good heavens, Mrs. Dow," Eldridge cried. "Are you hurt? My ladies, are you injured? I'm so sorry, I couldn't control—"

"It's all right," Mrs. Dow said, although she was clearly shaken. "I think we are unharmed."

The horses quieted, Harry leaned down next to Bess and gently rested his rough hand on her shoulder. "Are you all right, Miss? Does anything feel broken?"

"No, no," she managed to utter. "But my sister. Is she hurt?"

"No, Bess, I'm not hurt," Sarah said, but she began to cry, and Mrs. Dow wrapped her arms around her.

"Should I go for help?" one of the older stonemasons asked.

"No, that won't be necessary. We are just a bit shaken," Mrs. Dow said, gathering up her skirts and allowing one of the men to help her and Sarah to their feet.

"We didn't hear you coming," another man said.

"Of course not—it was an accident. Are the horses all right?" She turned to Eldridge.

He assured her they were, and three of the men got on one side of the carriage and righted it while Harry held firm to the horses' reins, lest they be spooked again. At the sound of the carriage landing, one of the horses snorted and shook his head and caught young Harry on the side of the face. He jumped back, and his hand flew up to his eye.

"Ouch!" Bess exclaimed sympathetically. "Is your eye injured?"

"No. It's fine," he said. "And besides, I have another one," he said, smiling. "I'm Harry Fletcher, by the way."

"I'm Bess Kent," she said. "You're sure your eyesight hasn't been impaired?"

"Not at all, it seems. I can see you perfectly. As a matter of fact, I think I've seen you before. In church, perhaps? Don't you live at Attwood Manor?"

"Why yes, I do." She had never noticed him before. He was tall, with dark, wavy hair a bit too long in the back and intense blue eyes. She guessed he was a few years older than she. She was certain she would have remembered if she had ever seen him.

"Your mother has the, ah, red hair," he said.

"She's not my mother, thank you," she said quickly.

"Come along, Bess," Mrs. Dow said as she settled herself and Sarah in the back of the righted carriage.

"Nice to meet you, Lady Bess," Harry said. "I'll see you in church."

"Just Bess," she said. "You can call me Bess."

Chapter Twenty

Mrs. Dow sat in the velvet wing chair by the south-facing window next to Bess's bed. The light was better there. Her eyes were not what they had been when she first came to fill the position of housekeeper at Attwood years ago.

With careful, tiny stitches she sewed the seam back together on Bess's mother's nightgown, the way she did every time it pulled apart.

"It's becoming quite threadbare," Mrs. Dow commented. "I don't know how much longer I'll be able to repair it."

Bess put down her knitting and rested her cheek on the pale blue nightgown. "I wear it every night." She lovingly rubbed the material between her fingers.

"I know." Mrs. Dow looked up over the wire spectacles that sat on the tip of her thin nose.

"It reminds me of Mummy," Bess said. "There's so little I have left of her now."

"I know that, too."

"I understand that Mummy has gone to heaven," Bess said, moving her head to Mrs. Dow's lap. "Everyone says so. And I include her in my prayers every night. It's just that I hadn't realized that she would be gone for so long. Day after day after day. That's the thing, I guess. I didn't realize how long forever was going to be. It just keeps going on, and there's no end to it."

~~~~~~~~~

The next morning, Bess sat cross-legged on the floor of the drawing room, carefully picking out the knots from her doll's hair and then dancing her across the carpet.

"I look wretched," she said as she pretended to speak for her doll. "I didn't get in from the ball till way past midnight."

Sarah's doll lay stretched out, facedown. "Get up, lazybones! We have to wash and dress and get off to the market."

Sarah slowly rolled her doll over, making her groan and reply, "Oh, all right. I am getting up. Fetch me some tea and scones with lots of jam."

Next to their father's study, with its huge globe of the world and stuffed tiger, the drawing room was the girls' favorite room to play in. They would line up their dolls and sit under the enormous oil painting of their mother. She had posed for the portrait when she was pregnant with her third baby. She and the baby had died in childbirth less than six months later. But in the portrait she looked young and vibrant as she leaned back, lovely in a cream-colored satin gown, her daughters sitting at her feet and Bess's arms crossed over her lap. Their mother's black hair was spun up on top of her head, and a gardenia was tucked behind her ear. Sarah's hair was dark, but Bess's was as black as a moonless night, just like her mother's. And Bess had the same flashing dark eyes as her mother that softened instantly when she was around her father, Sarah, or the dog.

Suddenly the door flew open, and Elsie appeared in the threshold.

"Good morning, girls," she said and waited for the reply she had insisted they give her when she addressed them.

"Good morning, Mother," they managed to squeeze out through gritted teeth.

Elsie was dressed in one of her poufy purple dresses, purple being her favorite color. Since she had married the duke, Bess noticed the color had begun to sprout up like weeds around the house. If a chair needed re-covering, it would suddenly reappear from the upholsterer covered in an eye-popping purple instead of the soft, lovely fabrics her mother had always chosen. When the sitting room off the kitchen needed repainting, it was finished in a color that Bess described as miserable mauve. No one sat in that room anymore except Elsie.

"I am off to the shops this morning," Elsie announced, adjusting her feathered hat. "What are you two doing?"

"Just playing," Sarah said. They fussed over their dolls, avoiding her chilly stare. Bess was eager to get back to the bottle and finally get it to Chap, but it had been raining hard all morning, and she knew Mrs. Dow wouldn't allow them to go out in such weather.

"Look at me when I speak to you," Elsie said.

The girls slowly raised their eyes. She wasn't a pretty sight. There was Elsie's explosion of bright red hair rising high above her chalky powdered face. Her small, pale blue eyes, set too close together, peered down at them.

She squinted hard at Bess's doll and a cool shadow of displeasure fell over her face. "What is that around her neck?" she asked.

"A cross." Bess tossed her dark braids back defiantly.

"I can see that. I'm not blind. Where did it come from?" Elsie demanded.

"It was my mother's. It's to be mine to wear when I'm eighteen. You know that."

"Yes, I do. And so do you. And last time I checked, you were twelve, not eighteen. Did you get into the family jewelry box and take that out?" Her voice rose as she frowned hard.

"I didn't think anyone would mind," Bess said.

"Well, I do mind. Give it to me. Now." Her voice rose and little red dots, the same color as her hair, appeared on her neck. "How dare you take jewelry out of the family box. How *dare* you, I say. Give it to me."

Bess's eyes filled up as she quickly slipped the gold cross off her doll's neck. "I'll put it back," she whispered and stood up.

"You'll do no such thing," Elsie insisted, sputtering and snatching the necklace from her hand.

"I won't have you anywhere near the box," she ordered, frowning at the necklace. "What happened to the pearl in the middle? It's missing. There are only thirteen pearls here, and there should be a fourteenth in the center."

"It's always been missing as far as I know," Bess

said. "Papa meant to get it replaced. I guess he hasn't had the time yet."

"Well, that's typical of your father," she said. "I'll deal with this. I won't say anything to your father this time, but if you do this again there will be serious consequences."

Gripping the cross, Elsie turned and spun out of the room, leaving behind only the scent of her perfume.

Chapter Twenty-One

The next time Bess saw Harry Fletcher, he was bouncing along atop a horse-drawn cart piled high with fresh hay. When he spotted Sarah and Bess marching up the drive to Attwood Manor, he pulled the horses to a stop along the road.

"Hello there, Ladies Kent!" he called out, tipping his hat.

"Harry! What are you doing up there?" Sarah shaded her eyes from the sun.

"Your groundsman hired me and two other lads from town to help him cut your fields."

"I thought you were a stonemason," Bess said.

"My father is a stonemason, and he's taught me well. But in these times, a fellow has to have a few trades if he's going to survive. You want a ride?" He patted the seat next to him.

"Won't we get all dirty?" Sarah started to complain, but Bess was already pulling her up with her.

"Well, the view is quite nice up here." Bess sat next

to Harry, and she wiggled over to make room for her sister.

"Yes, and I can see it a bit better now that my eye has healed," he said with a grin on his face.

"Ah, well, that's good to know." Bess tilted her head pleasantly. "Take us back up to the house, and I'll give you some tea for your trouble."

"After a long day in the hay fields, tea sounds like a fine idea," he quickly agreed. He looked her up and down and said, "I'm relieved to see you look none the worse for the carriage accident."

"Ha!" she exclaimed. "We Kents are a hardier bunch than that!"

Gertrude was busy polishing some items when they settled in the kitchen. She stopped what she was doing, washed her hands, and laid out warm scones, clotted cream, and a scoop of honey.

"Gertrude, you spoil us!" Bess gave the cook a loving squeeze while Sarah poured the tea for all of them.

"Gertrude," Bess said suddenly, eyeing the object the cook was buffing. "What are you doing with that?"

Freshly polished and hanging from the cook's fingers, Bess immediately recognized the pearl-encrusted cross that Elsie had taken from her.

"Just finishing up what Her Grace asked me to—"

"No. I mean the cross." Bess interrupted, waving her hand dismissively at the other items. "Why does she want you to polish that?"

"No special reason, my lady." Gertrude showed her the velvet box that she was to return it to. "I think once I've cleaned these things up, she wants to wrap them and put them back up in the attic and in the jewelry box. They were getting dirty and musty."

"All right," Bess said. She took the cross from Gertrude and laid it on the kitchen table to show Harry. "This was my mother's before she died," she announced proudly. "It's to be mine to wear when I'm eighteen. I treasure it."

"It's beautiful," he said, picking it up to examine it. "What do the letters engraved on the back stand for?"

"DSS J. K.," Bess said. "Duchess Julia Kent."

"You'll look beautiful wearing it," he said.

"But not until I am eighteen," Bess said, returning the cross to its box and then to Gertrude. "And not a day before," she said sarcastically. She realized she must sound bitter and changed the subject.

"Do you think you'll live on the island for the rest of your life?" Bess asked Harry.

"Well, I'm not really sure. I have so many things that I think I might want to try. Truth be told, I don't know what I'm meant to be in this world. I only just turned fourteen. I have some time to figure it all out," Harry said thoughtfully.

"Your true north," Bess said.

"What? What's that?" Harry asked, helping himself to another scone.

"What you were meant to be," she explained. "I used to ask my mother what she wanted me to be when I grew up, and she always told me she wanted to help me find my own true north. Not what people think you should be, but who you know you should be. Where your heart lies."

"And do you know your true north, Bess?" Harry asked, putting the last bite in his mouth.

"I do. I'm certain that I am destined to be an explorer like my father." She considered telling him about the bottle, but decided against it for now.

"Can girls be explorers?" he asked.

"I don't think whether one is a boy or a girl has anything to do with exploring. Why don't you meet me at the library tomorrow morning at eleven o'clock, and I'll show you some of the books that I've been reading. You will be astounded at what there is left to discover on this planet. You might find them interesting, or you might find some other subject that you like better. Who knows? Many people have discovered their true north by reading books, Harry. I plan on—" Bess stopped short as Elsie entered the kitchen.

"What is that dirty old hay cart doing out front?" Elsie interrupted, her long skirt swishing behind her. Bess felt her stomach clench.

"This is Harry Fletcher, Mother," Sarah replied. "He was one of the fellows who helped upright the horse cart when we were coming back from the village. We just ran into him out by our backfield. He's helping with the fall haying here at Attwood."

Harry jumped up and politely bowed his head. "Good day, Your Grace. It's a pleasure to meet you."

"Well, Harry needs a bath after his long day's work," Elsie said, sighing. "I'm sure his parents would want him to head home now." It wasn't a suggestion.

Before Bess could open her mouth, Harry calmly nodded. "I'll be going on now. Thank you for the tea. Bess, I'll see you at church if not before."

"I hope to see you tomorrow," she answered, both of them ignoring Elsie's slow boil.

"I'll try, if I get my chores done in time." He turned and walked calmly out the door, nodding to Bess at the last moment as he left.

"Whatever do you girls mean," Elsie said, "inviting

the son of a stonemason into our house. Perhaps I should speak to your father about having hired him to work on the property. The likes of him does not belong in our kitchen. After all—"

"If he's good enough to work at the Queen's estate, Mother," Bess replied, squaring off, "he is more than appropriate to work at Attwood."

Elsie and Bess glared at each other until Elsie finally picked up her skirts and sputtering to herself, clomped up the stairs.

Chapter Twenty-Two

Bess headed out earlier than usual the next afternoon. She made sure to pack her library books in a larger-than-necessary bag and hurried down to Singing Beach. She was relieved when she reached into the rocky opening where she and Sarah had hidden the bottle. It was just as they'd left it. Pulling it out, she inspected it before tucking it into her bag and hurrying off to the library.

The periodical section of the library had two large club chairs that faced each other with a long table in between. Bess returned last week's books and checked out five new ones, then sat with *Merry's Museum Magazine* spread out on the table. The magazine always arrived on the island a few months after being published in America, but the stories and letters were so exciting it didn't matter how late she read them.

She read a story called "The Chinese Wall."

There is not, perhaps, in the world a more stupendous work of art than the Great Wall, which marks the northern boundary of the Chinese Empire, dividing it from Tartary.

She made a mental note to add the Great Wall of China to her list of places to visit.

She would tell Papa every detail of the next story, "A Frightened Tiger."

You may talk about your lions—I have always said, and I always will say, that for pure blood-thirstiness and ferocity, the tiger is a far uglier beast than the lion. The tamest tiger that ever was, just let him snuff blood once, when he is hungry, and nothing can hold him!

"To think," she said out loud, "that my papa came face-to-face with such a beast!"

"So this is where you think I'll find my true north, do you?" Harry asked as he came up behind her.

"Well, hello there," she said. She jumped up, delighted that he came. "You might indeed find it here. You must read the stories in *Merry's Museum*, Harry. They are nothing short of thrilling, I promise.

"So now that you're here," she continued, "let's see what else we can come up with to interest you. Have you ever been to this library before?"

"Of course," he said. "Just not for a while. Well, come to think of it, not for a long while. So you be my guide, Lady Bess. Where do we start?"

He followed her over to the long rows of neatly sorted books.

"A," she pronounced, running her finger over the spines of several books. "A is always a good place to start. How about A for accountant?"

"Oh, I'm not too keen with numbers," he said, wincing.

"Well, A is also for astronomer or architect or apple picker!"

"Keep going," he said.

"Then you come, of course, to the letter B. Now there is baker."

"Well, I do like to eat," he pointed out.

"B also stands for beekeeper or butcher."

Harry cringed. "I'm allergic to bees and can't stand the sight of blood. Shall we move on to C? Actually, why don't you pick out a couple of books for me, and I'll see how it goes this week?"

She carefully chose a couple she thought he'd like— one about exploring and another all about London.

"And this is one of my favorites," she said, pulling out a biography of Marcus Aurelius. "I've read it so many times, I'm likely responsible for its worn cover."

Harry took it from her and opened the book to a random page. "Who is he?"

"He was a Roman emperor," Bess said. "But more importantly he was a philosopher. Read it, Harry, and I promise you will find at least one thing he said that will inspire you."

"'Waste no more time arguing about what a good man should be,'" Harry read, "'be one.' Hmm, I like that."

"See? You already found something!" Bess said gleefully and took the book from him. She slowly thumbed through it until she stopped and slapped the page she had been looking for. "This is one of Papa's and my favorites."

She cleared her throat and read slowly, bestowing the words with the reverence she felt they deserved. "'Do not act as if you had ten thousand years to throw away. Death stands at your elbow. Be good for something, while you live and it is in your power.'"

"I like that even better," Harry said. "I guess we all should try to live by that."

"Easier said than done. But now," she said, lowering her voice, "I'd like you to meet a friend of mine down at the dock. But I must have your word that you'll keep to yourself what I'm going to discuss with him."

"S," Harry said.

"S?" Bess asked.

"Yes, S. For secrets. I'm excellent at keeping them. So let's go meet your friend. I must admit I like the docks a bit better than the library."

Chapter Twenty-Three

Chap was waiting for Bess when she reached the *Land's End* with Harry by her side.

"Permission to board, Captain," she said. "Along with my friend, Harry Fletcher."

Although they'd never met, Harry had seen the older man around the village. A black man with wild silver curls and one blue eye was a memorable sight anywhere. Chap liked Harry right away, with his easy grin and straightforward manner, and they talked boats for a bit before Bess reached into her book bag and pulled out the bottle.

She told them how she and Sarah found it wedged in the sand at Singing Beach. They were all quiet for a few minutes after she showed them the paper about the slave and the carved heart.

"The first thing I'd say," Chap finally began, "is that there is nothing to indicate *where* this girl was born or lived. There is no way to even know if the paper is authentic."

"Why wouldn't it be?" Bess asked.

"People have been tossing bottles in the sea for years," he explained. "Sometimes with their name and address asking whoever finds it to write and tell them where it landed. It's a way to track currents, you see. And people on sinking ships sometimes write notes to a loved one and toss them overboard, hoping when and if it's found, the finder will send it on to the loved one. I don't know if that makes any sense for this one, though. A colored slave. Slavery has been illegal in Great Britain for years."

"It's still legal in the United States," Harry put in.

"It is." Chap scratched his wild gray head of hair and nodded, his expression darkening. "Yes, sorry to say, it is."

"Did you see or hear much about it when you were there, Chap?" Bess asked.

He touched the scar that ran like a jagged collar around his neck. "Seen it, lived it a bit. Hope never to have anything to do with it again."

Both Bess and Harry were speechless. The silence sat among the three until Chap finally said, "Well, I'm sure you're curious. Why wouldn't you be?"

"You don't have to say anything if you don't . . ." Harry began, trailing off.

"No, it's all right," Chap said, but his voice dropped. "It's not a secret. Maybe you should know—know about the way it is over there. I was born in New York a free black man. My father was an escaped slave, and my mother was Irish. That's where I get my blue eyes. Or 'eye,' I should say." He snorted with laughter.

"We lived on a farm near a lake where my father taught me to fish and farm. He's the one who taught me how to tie knots and to sail a boat. My ma made sure I could read and write. My father was so proud of that. He died when I was twelve, and my ma died the next year. I did my best to run the farm myself from then on till one day, out of the woods, come two white men with guns and ropes with their horse pulling a covered wagon. Got up close to me and something didn't seem right, so I started for my gun, but they jumped me first. That's when I saw what was in the back of their wagon. Black men. Each one chained to the other and to the floor of the wagon. The men were slave catchers. Come up North and took back as many blacks as they could snatch and sold 'em back South on the auction block."

Bess gasped. "But you were a free man, Chap!"

He raised his eyebrows and laughed. "I wouldn't

have been once they had me south of the Mason Dixon line. It wasn't uncommon for slavers to come north and grab free blacks, especially once slave boats stopped coming over from Africa."

"Did they get you South?" Harry asked, his cheeks afire at the injustice.

"They had four men in the back secured with chains. They ran out of chains for me. So they took rope and hog-tied my left wrist behind my back to my neck. I screamed and hollered and cussed at them. One of them finally said he'd shoot me then and there if I didn't shut up, and he tightened the ropes so they cut through my flesh. So I lay there until that night when they'd had enough whiskey and fell asleep."

"How did you get free?" Bess asked.

"No one can tie a knot—or untie one—better than Chap Harris," he said, tossing his head back defiantly.

"Did you free the others with you?" Harry asked.

"I didn't have the keys to their chains. I've always been sorry for that, but I had no choice. I wonder sometimes where they are now."

"Why didn't you go back to your farm?" Bess said.

"They would have just come back one day. Taken me again. I knew I couldn't go home again. Made my way to Boston and found work on the docks."

"You couldn't have been more than fourteen," Harry said. "Is that when you lost your eye?"

"No, that's a different story for another day," he answered, smiling.

Bess imagined what Harry was thinking. He had never been off the Isle of Wight. Chap's history seemed incredible.

"About fourteen. Yes, that's about right," Chap said. "Sort of stopped counting birthdays after my folks passed."

"How did you know how to go about getting a job once you were there?" Harry asked.

"I'd heard about Boston and New York City. I knew enough that they weren't in slave states and that they were big cities. A man can always find some work in a city if he's not choosy."

He shrugged his shoulders, his face like a tight knot. "And here I am."

"Now," he said, with no bitterness but as firm as Bess had ever heard him, "I don't mind telling you my story. But I don't want to tell it again. I'd be obliged if you didn't either. No one else's business, if you know what I mean."

Chapter Twenty-Four

Chap picked up the carving that had come out of Bess's bottle and twisted it toward the light.

"Now, so this little thing," Chap said as he held up the carved heart and laughed. "I'd like to tell you it is made of some precious stone, but I believe it is the pit of some fruit."

"Really?" Bess said, knowing that after Chap's story, her face must be as white as Chap's hair. She noticed that Harry's hands were trembling, and he tucked them under his arms. He was unable to stop staring at the scar gouged into Chap's neck.

"Yes," Chap continued. "People have made an art of carving fruit pits for centuries. You should see the intricate work I've seen some sailors do when they're at sea for months and have a lot of time on their hands. I'm not sure which fruit it came from. But I'd bet that's what it is. Not valuable, but an amusing little trinket. Lots of times they've been used like a worry stone. Know what that is?"

Bess and Harry looked blankly at him.

"Well now, that began back in ancient Greece. Take a little something about this size," he said, holding the heart between his index and thumb, "and you rub it. It's supposed to calm your mind and relieve your worries. Sometimes they were made out of precious stones and sometimes . . ." He held it up to make his point. ". . . sometimes they were made from the pits of fruit."

Bess carefully rolled the paper back up and dropped it in the bottle. But she tucked the carved heart in her pocket before plunging the cork back in the bottle. With Papa off traveling so much and having to deal with Elsie, Bess decided a worry stone would be a fine idea. She held the bottle up to let the sunlight flitter off its curves and said, "If Agnes May Brewster is indeed a colored slave in America, can you imagine how thrilled she might be to know her name has traveled all the way across the ocean? Maybe she is somewhere dreaming about where her name has been and where it might be going! Free as a bird."

"More like a fish," Harry said, shaking his head. "You're a hopeless romantic, Bess."

But Chap bit his lip and said, "She may find out for herself what it's like to be that free. Word is that in

America the North is fixing to fight the South if they don't make slavery illegal."

"A rebellion?" Bess asked, incredulous.

"Well," Chap went on, "most folks think it'll probably never come to that. But they're dead serious about freeing all the slaves. There was a lot of talk about it even a few years ago when I was still in Boston. There are many people fired up about it being against God's will and all."

"I don't know how I feel about a war, but it would be wonderful to think that my friend—" Bess hesitated, knowing it sounded a little silly to refer to a name on a piece of paper as her friend, "that Agnes May Brewster would be free!"

"And the moon," said Harry, "is made of green cheese, Bess."

"See here, Bess." Chap pointed at the bottle. "That cork won't be enough to protect the paper from the moisture on the island. You can see where there's wax still stuck around the lip of the bottle. That's probably why it made it from wherever it came from in such good condition."

"I know," she said, nodding. "It was sealed when I found it. I cut off the wax. If I leave it outside much longer, I shall seal it up again."

"D." Harry looked at Bess.

"D?" She asked.

"Yes, D. D for detective. Perhaps that should be the subject of your next book."

Bess stopped at Singing Beach on her way home and hid the bottle back in the alcove in the rocks, making a mental note to return soon with a candle to reseal the cork with wax. She kept the carved heart tucked in her pocket. *I think I'll need this*, she decided, rubbing it between her fingers.

Chapter Twenty-Five

Even this late in August, the air rolling in from the English Channel still blew warm over the island some days. But no one at Attwood Manor's long polished dining table could mistake the frosty air that hung between the duke and Elsie. "For the first time in months there were more people at the dock leaving the island than coming," the duke said as he finished his breakfast. His daughters sat on either side of him at the table, with Elsie at the opposite end. "It seems we've had more tourists this summer than ever before, don't you think?

"Not going to be this lovely weather much longer. What do you say we go off for a sail today, girls? Are you up for that?" he asked. "Probably the last chance we'll have this summer."

"Yes!" the girls both quickly agreed.

"May I invite Harry Fletcher, Papa?" Bess asked.

"I don't see why not." Despite Elsie's opinion, her father rather liked Harry Fletcher, who was spending more and more time at Attwood.

Elsie moved her food around her plate with little enthusiasm. She was subject to seasickness and never joined them on the boat.

"Would you like to give it another try, Elsie?" the duke asked.

"You know the answer already," she mumbled into her eggs and toast.

"Very well." The duke cleared his throat and waited while the maid poured him another cup of tea before making an announcement.

"I was in touch with the Royal Geographical Society when I last visited London," he began. "They have asked me to head up an important mission for the Crown."

"What is it, Papa? You're not going to India again, are you?" Sarah asked, practically popping up out of her chair.

"No, darling, not India. I have been asked to go to Africa. It is an enormous honor and an adventure. Perhaps the last great mystery on earth is to discover the source of the Nile River. Men have tried for centuries."

Elsie's spoon dropped into the middle of her plate. "Have you said yes?"

"Indeed. Yes, I have," he said firmly.

"Without even consulting me? Am I to be here

alone with all the responsibility for *your* children and this home?"

"The staff is well equipped to take care of Attwood Manor. I leave next week from Portsmouth," he said. "We sail to Zanzibar off the east coast of Africa. It is imperative that we go now before the rains come. I'm told that when it floods it is impossible to travel there."

"How long will you be gone, Papa?" Bess missed him already, and the thought of more long weeks alone with Elsie gave her no comfort. "Oh, Papa, won't you please at least consider taking me? I forgot to tell you that I have been reading all about Africa and India in *Merry's Museum Magazine* at the library. I've read that tigers are far fiercer than lions. I would be safe with you. Oh, please?"

"No, Bess, don't even make such a request. It is no place for a young lady. I'll be gone six months, I'm afraid. After we reach the island of Zanzibar, we'll gather up more supplies and hire on guides. From there we will ferry to the mainland and head west into the country looking to see if there is a specific river or mountain stream or lake that feeds the river.

"But I will write when I'm able. I'm told that porters carry messages back and forth from the bush when they can. Imagine the wonderful stories I will come back with," he said. Bess noticed that his eyes gleamed at the thought.

"Perhaps you'll bring back a stuffed lion to keep your stuffed tiger company! Can you imagine the maids, Papa?" Sarah threw her head back and laughed.

The girls were caught up in the reverie. Elsie sighed loudly and looked away, out the window.

"Well," the duke said, trying to break the tension. "Why don't you girls get dressed for the sail. I think Mother just isn't feeling well today."

"She doesn't seem to feel well most days," Sarah said under her breath.

"You girls go along and have Gertrude pack up a lunch, will you?" The duke nodded toward the doorway, and both girls, eager to avoid Elsie's sulking, quickly left.

"Gertrude will ask what Papa wants to drink," Sarah said as soon as they left the room.

"I'll go back and pop my head in to ask. You go ahead and have Gertrude start with the food." Bess turned back toward the dining room.

"Careful that you-know-who doesn't pop your head right off," Sarah said, disappearing down the stairs to the kitchen.

Bess stopped short outside the double dining room doors when she heard Elsie's voice trembling with rage.

"And what shall I do for money? You have me on such a budget that I can barely buy decent clothes!" Bess heard her stepmother whine. "Why, I am the talk of the village. Imagine a duke's wife who dresses no better than a common tavern maid."

"The accounts will all be taken care of and paid in my absence." Bess's father's voice had an edge to it that made her stomach clench. "As for your clothing allowance, Elsie, there simply is no extra money in the budget to cover any more."

"I thought when I married a duke . . ." Elsie's voice trailed off.

"My dear, there are many royals who are wealthy in land and title but must be frugal with their expenditures. I'm sorry that you are disappointed."

"Bitterly, I'm afraid," she said. Bess would listen no more. She couldn't bear to hear her father further humiliated by Elsie the Shrew. She picked up her skirts and quietly hurried away.

"And what does your father want me to pack for him to drink?" Gertrude inquired when Bess, pale faced, appeared in the kitchen.

"Please pack some sherry for him," Bess said quietly.

They spent the rest of the day sailing around the westernmost point of the island. Bess was pleased Harry had been able to join them. They took their time, and when they finally headed back to shore and Attwood the nightingales were singing by the light of the moon.

~~~~~~~~~~

On the morning of the duke's departure the following week, Attwood's staff stood in a row next to the front door, waiting to say good-bye to the master of the estate. Gertrude nervously twisted her apron. Bess figured she must be thinking about having to deal with Elsie in the duke's six-month absence. Sarah looked glum.

While the duke oversaw his valises being packed into the carriage, Elsie eyed Bess critically. "Oh, Mrs. Dow," Elsie said with a scowl. "Can't you do something with Bess's hair? She needs to start presenting herself better. It reflects poorly on me if she is running about the island with her hair loose. And she's always gnawing away at her nails." Elsie flipped up a lock of Bess's hair and then turned Bess's hands over, frowning at her nails.

"Well, I've taken to using a worry stone lately, and I find it very useful. I don't bite my nails nearly as much," Bess announced.

"A what?" Elsie asked.

"A worry stone," Bess stated. "People have used them since ancient times. You rub a small object that feels pleasing between your thumb and your index finger, and it helps to calm you and relieves stress and worry."

Bess was grateful when Mrs. Dow interrupted. "I think Bess has lovely hair, Your Grace. She just needs to remember to brush it up neatly more often. We'll work on that, won't we, Bess?"

"I suppose so," Bess reluctantly agreed. She was willing to say almost anything to get Elsie to leave her alone.

"Well, I believe everything is in good order." The duke stood back, looking at the carriage stuffed with valises and crates packed with maps and charts.

"Are you certain it will take six whole months to find the silly headwaters of the Nile River, Papa?" Bess asked, eager to change the subject from her appearance. "Study your maps carefully, and I think you can succeed in less time." She tenderly patted the sleeve of his jacket. "Sarah and I shall miss you so awfully."

"It's quite a task, but I'll try," he vowed. "I shall write you the minute the ship reaches Zanzibar."

"I have borrowed books from the library about it.

Zanzibar seems to be a colorful place," Bess said, before blowing her nose into a hankie. "And watch out for lions, Papa. If you should see one, stare it down bravely."

"Good advice, my dear. I will heed it." With one daughter clinging to each side of him, he reached out for Elsie, but she stood frozen in her spot.

"Well, then," he said to her. "Take care of yourself, my dear."

She nodded and said, "We'll look for your correspondence."

With that, the duke climbed into the carriage driven by Eldridge. Bess ran and waved behind him, and watched glumly as he disappeared down the driveway toward the docks and the ship that would take her dear papa first to Portsmouth and then to the darkest corners of the world.

Chapter Twenty-Six

Whenever Chap told Bess and Harry tales of his worldly adventures, Harry would, in turn, regale them with the stories his uncle Alfie had told him. Alfie Fletcher had been a constable in London's seamy East End for twenty years, and his stories would raise the hair on a bald man's head. Gruesome murders to solve, wretched thieves with knives at the ready, even abandoned street children who roamed the alleys and garbage piles. Bess, who had only been off the island once with her papa, was spellbound. She secretly resolved to do what she could to help people when she was older—in between her exploring. She was determined to be good for something, as Marcus Aurelius advised.

After dealing with the murdering thieves that inhabited the dark side of London, Harry told them that his uncle Alfie had jumped at the offer to move himself and his missus to the Isle of Wight to become chief constable of the quiet island. It was like a holiday compared to London, Harry said his uncle claimed. These days, Alfie rarely had to deal with more than an occasional misdemeanor or incident of rowdiness.

"Other than that," Harry told them, "the worst Uncle Alfie has to handle now is the occasional escape from Parkhurst Prison. About once a month, one of the young prisoners finds a way to escape. But there's no easy way to get off the island without a boat, and Uncle Alfie always manages to capture and return the poor fellow within twenty-four hours.

"He always feels a little sorry," Harry said, "because he knows that their punishment is a week down in the dark cells. They're not all bad, you know. Some of the boys are there for pickpocketing or public fighting, and some just because they have no family and no money."

So the morning that Mrs. Dow answered the rap at the front door, and Bess heard the visitor introduce himself as Constable Alfie Fletcher, she flew down the hall to meet him. Elsie followed closely behind.

"Good morning, Your Grace," he began. "Allow me to introduce myself. I am Chief Constable Alfie Fletcher."

"Yes? What is your business here, sir?" Elsie asked, waving both Bess and Mrs. Dow away. Mrs. Dow quietly disappeared down the hall, but Bess didn't move. *He doesn't look as fearsome as I had imagined*, she thought, examining him up and down.

"I have here a letter I received from the police in Westminster Borough in London," Alfie explained. "They have arrested a fellow running a pawn shop there who was selling stolen goods."

"Whatever would that have to do with us?" the duchess asked.

"Well, they inventoried a list of items that they believe might have been stolen, and there were some pieces that have been traced back to the Kent family. For instance, a sterling silver tea service has been identified by the Kent family coat of arms engraved on the back. And there was an oil painting of this house, identified by an art dealer as having come from your collection. Have any of these things been stolen?" Alfie closed his notebook and leaned one hand against the column. Bess wished Elsie would ask him in out of the sun. Maybe offer him a cup of tea. She had several questions she wanted to ask him about his days on London's police force.

"Stolen? Oh, my, why, I don't know. My husband has a vast amount of things in the attics here." She waved her arm toward the ceiling.

"Well, perhaps I should wait and speak to him when he returns," Alfie suggested.

"You will have to wait a long time for that," Bess interrupted. "My papa will be gone six months or more. He is off on an African expedition for the Queen."

"Ah, yes, I see, then," he said. Bess was surprised that Alfie was a heavy man. She figured he had probably gained weight since he had stopped rushing around London chasing down all kinds of riffraff. Bess could see beads of sweat gathering between the rolls of fat on his neck.

"Well, is there an inventory of the family's valuables?" he asked.

"You know," Elsie said, "now that you mention it, I have noticed a few things missing. I thought perhaps they were misplaced, but now I wonder."

"Really?" Bess interjected. "You have? What? I haven't noticed anything, Mother."

Elsie glared at her stepdaughter. "Bess, dear," she said, "why don't you go to your room and make sure nothing is missing there." When Bess didn't move, Elsie leaned down, grasped her shoulders, turned her around, and hissed, "Shoo! Go on upstairs now."

Elsie waited while Bess slowly climbed the stairs. She went to her bedroom and opened and closed the door. But instead of going in, she crept along the wall to the top of the stairs where she could hear the conversation below. *Elsie would make a terrible explorer*, she thought, *I would never fall for something so transparent as this!*

"Has there been anyone around who isn't ordinarily here? Anyone new in your employ who you might suspect?" Alfie picked up his questioning where he'd left off.

"No, no one in our employ. But . . ." Elsie hesitated.

"Ma'am, please speak freely to me," he urged.

"Well, there is one person . . . ." Her voice got quieter, and Bess had to strain to hear her.

"Yes? Go on," he said. Despite Elsie's attempt to keep the conversation discreet, Alfie's voice was deep and loud and carried quite nicely up to where Bess crouched.

"Of course you know all of the members of the Fletcher family?" the duchess asked.

"Yes, yes. Andrew Fletcher is my brother."

"And Harry is your nephew, then," she replied coyly.

"We are a fine family, I can assure you of that! Good grief, what would any of us have to do with anything from Attwood, Your Grace?"

"It's the boy. Harry." Elsie said. Bess stifled a gasp.

Could she be serious? It took all Bess had not to fly down the stairs to defend her friend.

"He has been coming here a good deal lately to visit with my stepdaughter. Now that I think of it, I caught him one day coming down the stairs from the attic. I asked him what he was doing there, and he simply ignored me, brushed past, and rushed out the door."

"Was he carrying anything with him?" Alfie asked.

"It took me quite by surprise, Constable, so I can't really say. It's possible," Elsie said.

"I just can't believe this, Your Grace. He's a fine boy. Is there anyone else—anyone at all—who you might suspect?"

"No," she said coolly. "Only Harry Fletcher."

Bess's pulse thumped in her throat, and she covered her mouth with her hands as her breathing grew louder.

"Well, I'll stop by and have a word with my brother. In the meantime, please check to see if anything else is missing from the attic, and let me know if you discover something. It's possible that the items were sold off or given away years ago and just now are turning up," he said nervously. "Perhaps nothing to get ruffled about."

"When my husband returns, I don't want him bothered with all this. Now will that be all, sir?"

"Ah. Yes, then. I won't be bothering you again. Good day."

Bess well knew that a scandal of this magnitude would not only ruin Harry, but it was unlikely that the island would keep Alfie on as constable if his family was associated with something like this. She couldn't imagine Harry locked up in Parkhurst Prison, its dismal gray walls broken only by small grated windows. She was certain that Alfie Fletcher left Attwood that day wanting the whole matter dropped.

Oh, what an evil devil you are, Elsie, Bess thought as she inched quietly away from the top of the stairs.

Chapter Twenty-Seven

On a clear, warm October day, Bess and Sarah watched as the postman pedaled his bike up Attwood's drive to deliver the mail. The staff gathered, and the girls ran in from outside. *Finally*, thought Bess, *a letter from Papa.* Elsie slit open the envelope and read her husband's careful hand out loud to the group.

September 21, 1855
My dear Elsie, Bess, and Sarah,
We sailed around the great Horn of Africa last week and arrived yesterday on the island of Zanzibar, located just off the east coast of this great Dark Continent.
The view as we approached was quite extraordinary. Minarets of Zanzibar's mosques stood out against the sky above the Sultan's palace. A sea breeze carried the scent of cloves and the beaches shimmered with white coral sands.
After registering with the British Consul here

we quickly pulled together a fine caravan of twenty native porters, two buffaloes, a camel, five mules, and five donkeys.

While we were disembarking from our ship, we were dismayed to see traders loading up their ships with the bounty they had gathered here. Humans. Black African human beings. Captured, chained together, and loaded like cargo to be taken to America and sold at the slave markets. It raises my fury as the international slave trade was supposed to end in 1808. Yet here in East Africa, the traders ignore the laws and continue to trade in human beings with little concern for any consequences. I watched as they also loaded huge ivory elephant tusks on their ships. There is a great demand for the material so we Europeans can have ivory piano keys, knife handles, and cameo broaches. One of the slaves, a very young boy, accidentally dropped one of the heavy tusks as he carried it up the gangplank. A burly man pulled back his whip and lashed the lad until he fell into the water.

"Let that be a warning to the savages to take care with our ivory," the man said while he laughed. Words fail me to describe how disturbing *it is to see how, in pursuit of money, these traders have virtually no regard for life.*

I shall be glad to leave this island behind and travel into the country. I look forward to the unspoiled beauty of the land.

We are almost finished loading up our supplies and will engage an additional six porters just to carry the beads and colorful cloth that we will trade with the natives for fresh food or for the ability to pass through their territories.

We set out tomorrow by ferry to the mainland, and I am told that I will be able to get letters out to you over the next week. After that I expect we will be so deep into the heart of Africa that I will not be able to send many more communications.

What an adventure I am privy to here, my lovely ladies. The source of the great River Nile has eluded man for centuries. I have a good feeling about this.

> *Pray for our success,*
> *Papa*

Bess quietly prayed for him the first thing every morning and the last thing each night. It occurred to her that poor Agnes May Brewster could have been a slave on one of those boats and thrown her bottle over the side of the ship. But then she realized that she would not have been born with such an Americanized name, nor would the birth note have been written in English. The more she thought about it the more convinced she became that Agnes May was indeed a slave born on an American plantation. She added her to her daily prayers.

~~~~~~~~~~

Gertrude was nowhere to be found the next morning when Bess came down for tea and breakfast. But hearing hushed conversation coming from the kitchen, she stopped short—Elsie was talking with a man whose voice she didn't recognize. She tiptoed up to the pantry and stood behind the door where she could see and hear every word through the crack. She caught her breath when she saw Elsie at the kitchen table with several pieces of the Kents' sterling-silver service spread out before her and a pudgy little man with round spectacles and red suspenders carefully picking over each piece. Bess hadn't seen this silver for a long time. Along with many family treasures, they had been carefully stored away up in the attic.

"Hmmm," the man muttered. "Very nice. These

have been in the Kent family for many generations, I am sure." He turned each item over and carefully examined the engraved marking on the back. Many of them, Bess knew, bore her mother's or father's family crest.

"Oh, yes, indeed," assured Elsie.

Bess wanted to rush from her hiding place and scoop up her family's heirlooms from their grimy little paws. What were they doing?

"These will fetch a handsome price in London on Bond Street. Would you like me to pay you in pounds, Your Grace?" the man asked.

"That will do nicely," Elsie replied. "And remember, do not go back to the shop where you sold the tea set and painting! You must be more careful where you place these things. Only use the most discreet buyers. I cannot risk having items traced back to me again."

"Don't concern yourself. I will be the very picture of discretion," he assured her.

With that, the Bond Street dealer reached into his leather satchel and counted out several bills, which Elsie tucked into the watch pocket of her skirt. He left with the sterling that had been in Bess's family for more than a hundred years.

As he hustled off, Bess snuck away, furious and shaking, leaving her stepmother to count her money.

Harry, eh? Bess thought bitterly. She quickly realized it would be best to wait for Papa to come home to reveal what Elsie was up to. He would know what was missing from the attics and could follow up on the fellow from Bond Street. She knew that going against her stepmother probably wouldn't work. It never did. But she was hopeful. *Perhaps*, she thought, *Papa will finally see Elsie for what she is and banish her from our lives.*

Chapter Twenty-Eight

There was no fanfare when the Duke's second letter arrived. The girls found it on the table by the front door when they came home from doing errands in the village on a late October day. It had been opened, and they could smell Elsie's perfume on its pages.

"It's as if she doesn't even miss him!" Sarah said sadly.

"I am not so sure he misses her either," Bess answered before slowly reading every word aloud.

September 26, 1855
My dear Elsie, Bess, and Sarah,
We are only beginning our expedition and already the things I have witnessed leave me breathless. First the sunrise. The sun doesn't just rise in Africa. It bursts up from the horizon in the most brilliant crimson color you can imagine, and a rosy gold washes over the earth. It lasts a short while before the sun fully rises, and then the blistering heat sets in.

Last night we reached a small river and camped nearby. Porters had to stand guard by the river all night, as it is infested with huge, ferocious, man-eating crocodiles that slither out of the water silently when they think an easy meal is near. Joshu, one of the porters, told me that his mother and little sister were both taken by crocs as they approached the river to bathe, gather water, and wash clothes.

I'm told they snap their giant jaws around a person's middle and drag them under water to drown them in what the natives call a "death roll." The beast thrashes wildly until its victim succumbs, and after it's eaten its meal, it stores what's left of the body in underwater tree roots so it may return when it's hungry again. Gruesome business! I must confess, I do not sleep well near water here.

We also came across the rotting carcasses of five large elephants, all missing their ivory tusks. We assumed the traders we saw when we first arrived or others like them had slaughtered them. It was very sad, as there were two little baby elephants trying to get their mothers to stand up. They would not leave and made the most sorrowful moans. I asked one of our guides what would happen to the little ones without their parents to protect them, and he told me lions and hyenas would take them within days. I question the value of those combs, canes, knives, and jewelry made of ivory.

I cannot help but wonder why our Lord bothers to make so much beauty and then allows it to be so violently destroyed.

I am growing quite fond of Joshu. He is approximately thirty years of age and as black as a starless night sky. He is quite bright and knows a bit of English. It turns out he has led several expeditions before. He is, as I explained, motherless. His father was stolen by slave traders years before his mother was eaten, and he presumes the poor man is picking cotton on some Southern plantation in the United States.

As for our progress, we hope that by mapping out a fair piece of land around Lake Victoria, even if we are not successful in finding the river's source, we will have made it a great deal easier for the next explorers who come here.

I will end now as it has begun to rain and the porter who is to return to the coast must leave immediately. We few Brits send him off with our letters home.

I hope this reaches you all safe and well. I look forward to returning to England by the first of March. I shall bring lovely gifts from Africa for all my girls. Until then, take care of one another.

Pray for our success,
Papa

As she did each night before sleep, Bess prayed that the next day might be a good one for her father and that he would be safe, the Lord watching over him. She included her now-nightly prayer for Agnes May, and tonight, for the first time, she asked her Heavenly Father to please watch over the elephants, too.

Chapter Twenty-Nine

"If I prepare toast with strawberry jam, will you eat that?" Gertrude asked. "At least a mouthful? You need to have something for your breakfast." Bess knew she was troubling Gertrude and that she needed some nourishment. For the last week, she hadn't had an appetite, and more often than not, the cook caught her staring off into space, fighting back tears. Bess wondered again if anyone would believe her over the duchess if she told about Elsie selling things off. Papa would, she knew. With each passing day, she was even more certain her best hope was to wait for his return to expose Elsie.

"You know, my lady, if I may be so bold, I lost my own mother when I was about your age," Gertrude confided. "Got farmed out to be a servant when my own father couldn't take care of my brothers and me."

Bess patted Gertrude's hand. "That's kind of you to share, Gertrude."

"Just made these this morning," the cook said, nudging a plate of still-warm scones in front of Bess.

"I'm really not hungry," Bess said softly, rolling her carved heart between her thumb and index finger. "But thank you."

"Well, if you change your mind." Gertrude placed a tea cloth over the plate and left it on the table.

"What is that you're fiddling with?" she asked as Bess rolled the trinket absentmindedly between her fingers.

"My worry stone," Bess answered.

"Looks like an old fruit pit to me," Gertrude said.

"Hmm. I guess many things look like one thing to some people and quite another to someone else," Bess mused, staring off.

Gertrude shook her head and chuckled. "Well, now you've lost me. But if it makes you happy, it's not causing any harm."

Bess pushed around the plate of scones until something in the corner of the kitchen caught her eye.

"What's this?" she asked, eyeing a box next to the back door near the pantry. Crumpled pieces of old newspaper stuck out of the top.

"Her Grace placed it there," Gertrude answered. "Same as she did with a box last week. Since His Grace left, she's put one out every two weeks or so for some fellow who arrives on a Tuesday."

Bess tucked the carved heart in her watch pocket,

bent down next to the box, and unwrapped the newspaper. She recognized pieces of Kent family crystal that had been stored in the attic.

A small oil painting was tucked underneath the crystal. On the bottom were two tiny velvet cases. The first one contained a pair of her late mother's ruby earrings. She froze when she opened the second one. It contained the pearl-encrusted gold cross that Elsie had taken from her doll's neck. She turned it over and looked at her mother's initials, DSS J. K., engraved on the back. It was one of the last things that bound her to her mother. Shaking with rage, she carefully rewrapped everything except the small case that held the cross, which she tucked into her pocket. She took the box and disappeared to hide it in one of the unused rooms in the back of the house.

As she left, she looked at Gertrude and put her finger to her lips.

The cook stared down into the stewpot she was stirring and nodded, murmuring, "I didn't see a thing."

～～～～～～～

"When she finds out you took the box she'll be so angry." Sarah ran alongside her sister later that morning as they pushed down the path toward Singing

Beach. Rain had fallen all through the night, muddying the fields.

"And what is she going to say to Papa when he returns? 'I was selling off your family's heirlooms and Bess caught me?' She won't say anything, Sarah. But I won't let her sell anything else, and she cannot sell Mummy's cross. She can't have it! Wait till Papa returns and I tell him what she has been up to."

"Oh, Bess, what if she tries again to get Harry in trouble?" Sarah cried. "I couldn't stand that."

"I know, Sarah." Bess's voice was full of resolve. "We've both grown very fond of our Harry Fletcher."

"She'll go through your things and find it," Sarah said. "She always does. She snoops through everything."

"Let her snoop," Bess said defiantly.

"What are you going to do?"

"You'll see soon enough," Bess said, rushing along the paths so quickly that Sarah was having difficulty keeping up.

"Where did you put the box?" Sarah asked. "She'll demand you tell her where you hid it."

"In one of the guest-bedroom closets. Maybe I'll tell her about the box, but never Mother's cross," Bess said. "Keep the matches and the candle dry, Sarah. That's your duty." Bess had tucked an old white candle and several matches inside a bag and stuffed them inside Sarah's dress before sneaking out the back of Attwood.

They ran through the orchards where the apple trees, shrouded in November fog, loomed like gray ghosts. They reached Singing Beach just as dark clouds began to appear over the ocean and whitecaps raced across the surface. They would have to complete their task quickly. If it started to storm in earnest they would be expected to return to the house immediately, or someone would be sent to fetch them. Bess removed the rocks from the little cave and pulled out the bottle with Agnes May Brewster's name on the torn paper still rolled up inside. After pulling out the stopper, she closed her eyes, kissed the engraved gold cross on its chain, and dropped it inside the bottle, tightly re-corking it.

"What about the carved heart, Bess?" Sarah's eyes were wide.

"Elsie wouldn't care about that, but I do. It must have meant something to Agnes May. I won't keep her name hostage much longer, but I'm saving her heart so I always remember her. She must be very courageous. I'll carry her heart close to mine to remind myself that I, too, must be just as courageous."

"You think she really is a colored slave, then?" Sarah asked.

"I think it's a reasonable possibility. Now hand me the bag, Sarah, and hold the bottle sideways. Hold it steady."

Sarah did as she was told and watched as Bess struck the first match, held it to the candle's wick, and let the melted wax drip over the bottle's cork.

"Don't drop hot wax on my hand, Bess."

"Then stop shaking, and you'll have nothing to worry about."

"What will you do with it now?" Sarah asked.

"I don't know—I need time to think. I'll put it back in the nook for the time being. But I've been worrying about the damp and the rain. Chap says one reason it made it intact from wherever it came from is because it was sealed well with cork and wax. I won't let anything happen to it."

Bess tucked the sealed bottle far back in the little cave, then pulled Sarah along by the hand as they raced back to Attwood.

Chapter Thirty

Elsie appeared in the kitchen that afternoon as Gertrude was putting a lid on the evening's stew. Bess was sitting at the table sipping a cup of tea and working on her knitting. Her heart wasn't in it, but Mrs. Dow insisted the girls keep to their regular schedule while their father was away.

"Bess, what are you doing down here again? You seem to enjoy the kitchen more than any other room," Elsie asked, annoyed.

"I came to get myself a cup of tea and keep Gertrude company," she answered, counting stitches on her needle.

"We have servants to bring you your tea, Bess. And don't ruin your appetite. Perhaps you should take your knitting upstairs."

Bess raised her index finger to indicate she was counting stitches.

"Gertrude," Elsie said, turning to the cook, "I have a gentleman coming to discuss some small farming matters with me. When he arrives, I'd like to be alone with him in the kitchen so—" She stopped short.

"Where is the box I placed here?" she asked, her words coming out slowly.

"I, I don't know, Your Grace," Gertrude lied.

Elsie bent down, her long pointy nose almost touching the cook's, her unblinking eyes inches away from Gertrude's. "Where is it? Tell me. Now."

Wringing a dishcloth between her hands, Gertrude blurted out, "Bess took it this morning, ma'am. I had nothing to do with it at all!"

The color drained from the duchess's face as she turned slowly to face Bess.

"And what did you do with it?" Elsie asked, her lips pursed and twitching.

Bess put down her knitting and stood up to face her stepmother. "The question seems to be, Mother, what exactly were you planning on doing with it?"

Ignoring the question, Elsie asked, "Does this mean you aren't going to tell me where it is?"

"Well," Bess said, "I shall tell you this much. Harry Fletcher hasn't taken it."

They stood glaring at each other. Though unspoken, they both knew that the girl would tell her father everything when he returned.

A short time later, Elsie appeared in the kitchen again. "Have Eldridge bring the carriage around to the front," she ordered Gertrude, wrapping a lavender shawl over her bony shoulders.

"Where are you going?" Bess asked, trying to keep the alarm from her voice.

"None. Of. Your. Business," Elsie hissed.

"What about the fellow coming for the meeting, Your Grace?" the cook asked.

"When he comes, tell him I'm sorry, but something unexpected came up," Elsie said. "I'll be in touch with him later."

When the carriage pulled around to the front of the house, Bess watched with growing distress as Elsie briskly walked out and settled herself in the back.

"Take me to town. To the Constable's Office," Bess heard her order Eldridge.

~~~~~~~~~

When Constable Alfie Fletcher showed up at his brother's house an hour after Elsie's visit, Bess was already there. Alfie's whole body seemed to have sagged into itself, and he cried along with Harry's mother when he put handcuffs on Harry.

"I told her," Alfie said. "I says to Her Grace—'my

nephew has never been in trouble in his life. My brother and his family, they are good folks, ma'am.'

"'Not so good that he minds stealing from the very house where my stepdaughters have made him feel welcome,' she says back to me," Alfie said.

"This is all a lie, Uncle!" Harry yelled, enraged.

"Sir," Bess spoke up. "My stepmother is lying. It is she that is taking things from Attwood. Harry would never do such a thing."

"Do you have evidence of that, my lady?" Alfie asked.

"You have my word, sir!" Bess cried indignantly. "I could identify the man she is selling them to!"

"Please, miss," he said wearily. "Don't take offense. But your say-so against the duchess's? How old are you? She'll just say that you're trying to protect your friend. She even claims to have seen him. And why would the buyer admit to anything?

"Says she suspected him all along. Says last week when he was at the manor she looked out the window after he said good-bye to you. Says she watched as he snuck back in and up to the attic. Claims she saw him slip back down with a silver set under his arm and a small oil painting in his hand."

Harry's father interjected. "Why wouldn't she have

said something then, right away when it happened?" Raw fury caused his voice to crack.

"Claims she was terrified, her husband away and all. She insists that I arrest Harry immediately and have him locked up in Parkhurst Prison where he'll be no threat to her or her stepdaughters."

"Oh, my Lord." Harry's mother fell weeping against her husband. "Parkhurst Prison?"

"She even brought up the Queen." Alfie went on, sweating profusely now. "'What would our Queen do if she thought you were allowing a thief to roam around the island simply because he is your nephew?' she asked me."

"Where is the evidence beyond her word? Where is the silver and painting now?" Harry's father angrily demanded, slamming his hand on the table. "This is lunacy! You've only this woman's word, Alfie! Harry would never do such a thing."

"I've seen the items in a box in our house. And I would know if he had ever been in the attic," Bess argued. "He has never even been above the ground floor. Surely you believe us."

"I have no choice," Alfie said with a heavy heart. "She is the Duchess of Kent. Harry's word means very little next to hers. Have you seen Harry with anything at all that looks like it might have come from Attwood?"

"Are you out of your mind? Of course not!" Harry's mother said, beginning to sob louder. "I tell you this is not true. It can't be!"

"This is just outrageous. The duchess is lying—I swear to it!" Harry pleaded, his whole body trembling with anger and indignation.

"I'm telling you, too, Harry didn't do this!" Bess cried in frustration.

But the duchess had signed a complaint that said she'd seen him with her very eyes. And everyone knew that Alfie couldn't afford to lose his job. So despite the boy's angry protests, Bess's support, and his parents' pleas, Alfie Fletcher reluctantly deposited his frightened nephew in the infamous Parkhurst Prison.

Chapter Thirty-One

"How could you?" Bess burst into Attwood's drawing room a while later. Fueled by anger, she had run all the way from the Fletchers' cottage. She found Elsie completely concentrated on painting some flowers.

"I didn't hear you knock," Elsie said, not looking up. She was admiring the colors of the leaf and petals on her painting.

"Harry Fletcher stole nothing!" Bess raged. "I demand that you have him released from Parkhurst!"

This made Elsie giggle. "You demand? You are so amusing, dear! Oh, but I think not. Young Harry will be sent to the penal colony in Australia where he belongs."

"I shall tell everything I know. It's you who has been looting the family treasures. Not Harry. You can't get away with this! It's been you all along."

"Oh, my goodness, who would ever believe such a thing?" Elsie put a dab of sap green on one of the leaves.

"Gertrude, for one," Bess said. "She knew there were boxes there every week. Gertrude will vouch for it."

"Oh, dear. Didn't I tell you? Gertrude is gone. I let her go just after I came back from the Constable's office. All those creamy chowders and such—too rich for my figure. I had Eldridge take her in the carriage headed to the docks. Booked her ticket on a boat to Portsmouth and sent her off with a letter of recommendation. I'm hiring a lady from town who used to cook for the Cat and Mouse Tavern. She has excellent references. But Gertrude. Oh, my. Well, Gertrude is long gone. Her boat is probably halfway to Portsmouth at this very moment."

For the first time she looked up from her painting at Bess. In a steely voice she said, "You do see that it will be your word and the word of a lowly stonemason's son against mine. Not very good odds for you, I'm afraid. I won't quarrel with you any longer. Please close the door behind you."

Bess's hands were in tight fists, trembling at her sides. She wanted to grab Elsie's silly little painting and smash it on the floor. But she also knew that raging and pleading would not free Harry Fletcher. In all the adventure books she had ever read, the only way to succeed against evil was to be at least as calm and calculating as the villain you faced.

Bess willed herself to take a deep breath, took full measure of the enemy in front of her, and closed the door behind her.

When Chap's boat pulled up to the dock the next morning, Bess was waiting for him, pacing.

"And it's not even Thursday! To what do I owe this pleasure?" He hopped off the boat and began tying the ropes to the dock.

"It's Harry Fletcher," Bess blurted out.

She could barely tell the story straight, standing there in the cold shadow of Parkhurst Prison, knowing Harry was locked up inside its bleak walls. She willed herself not to fall down in a heap and cry.

"Ah, Bess." Chap whistled and shook his head slowly when she'd finished explaining. "A duchess against a poor stonemason's son. I'm sorry to tell you this, but he doesn't stand a chance. He's not the first innocent boy to be put in Parkhurst, and he won't be the last one."

"What will they do with him?" Bess cried.

"Unfortunately, they will probably put him on the boat like the rest of the lads. First Monday of every month, the ship pulls in, loads up the prisoners and takes them off either to stand trial in London or to the penal colonies on Australia or New Zealand."

It was too much, and she found herself sobbing on his shoulder.

"I must get him out," she said as she wept.

"Now be serious, girl. How are you going to do such a thing? Even if you could, they'd find him. Every so often some lad takes off, but they always find him within a day or two. Where can he go? Unless he can steal a boat, he's stuck on the island and surely someone would notice if he tried to leave. What a shame," he said, shaking his head. "No place for the poor boy. No place for any human being.

"Have they let you visit him yet?" he asked.

"No. I'm allowed to see him for ten minutes later this morning—at 11:30," Bess said.

She took his rough hand in hers and pleaded to him. "You could get him out. You have a key to the back door. Oh, Chap. You could put him on your boat and sail him over to the mainland. You had to leave those men chained to that wagon all those years ago. You had no choice then, but you have a choice this time. You don't have to leave Harry."

She searched his eyes and saw she'd struck a chord. But he didn't say so.

"Ha! I come marching out the back of Parkhurst Prison with a prisoner and just stroll on down to my boat?" he reasoned. "There are too many people around the docks at all times of the day and night. They'd see me with him. Bess, you aren't thinking straight."

"Yes, yes, of course." She sat down. She needed to

have her wits about her. She needed to quiet her heart and let her head take over. "But I need your help. Please."

She pulled a knotted handkerchief from her skirt pocket, opened it, and held up a double strand of pearls with a gold clasp.

He practically jumped back away from her. "Aye! You're not going to ask me to get in trouble for stealing from the duke, too!"

"They're not my father's. They're mine. I keep them in my jewelry box, and I can do with them what I wish. I wish to give them to you in exchange for your help. Chap, they will not buy you a palace, but they should fetch enough on Bond Street to pay to repair your boat. And perhaps enough will be left over to let you sail off somewhere else. To one of the places you always talk about going if you weren't stuck here."

"I don't want your pearls, Bess." Chap shook his head, his one blue eye staring straight at her.

"I have other strands of pearls, Chap. I've only worn these once. No one will ever notice. And when I'm eighteen I'll receive several more. I don't need these. But I do gravely need your help."

He dragged his fingers through his silver hair and visibly shuddered at the thought of prison. "Every day I take the buckets of fish up there, I feel my stomach clench. To lose your freedom—it's not the kind of thing that ever leaves you," he said.

By the time she paid a visit to Harry in Parkhurst later that morning, their plan was well laid.

Chapter Thirty-Two

Bess's heart was already pounding as she slipped out the back gate of Attwood two nights after her visit to Chap. Her hair was pulled back tight, and she wore a scarf so that in the event someone saw her, she would be harder to identify.

She had never been out by herself at this hour, let alone traveled down the dark, deserted lanes. Chap said it was important they do it when there was no moon, since they would be harder to spot. But they needed to act soon, while Harry was still being kept in the quarantine section of the prison. Once he was moved into the regular population, he would be securely locked up in one of the cells.

Bess was prepared to duck into the woods if she met someone, but the island was asleep at this hour, and she was alone the entire way. Creeping along the edge of the cliffs behind Parkhurst Prison, she saw Chap's boat steering away from the dock. She didn't have much time.

Fumbling in her pocket, Bess pulled out the key Chap used when he delivered fish to the prison and slipped it into the lock, turning it slowly. It seemed to her like the clink it made when the bolt flipped open could be heard from the docks. She stood silently for a moment, waiting to hear if someone was coming. Nothing. She edged the door open just enough to slip in, stole silently down the hall into the kitchen, and rapped once on the door to the boys' quarantine room.

The door opened partway, and Harry's face immediately rose up in front of her. She almost screamed, but he reached out and put his hand on her mouth and slid through the opening and into the kitchen.

"I was so afraid you wouldn't come," he whispered, his hands shaking.

She didn't answer. They both turned and moved quickly down the dismal, dank passageway and out the door.

"Wait," she said. She locked the door behind them with the key. "Now let's go."

They traveled in the opposite direction of the docks so they wouldn't be spotted. Stealing along the beaches wherever they could, they bent down low next to the bushes. But when the cliffs were too steep, they were forced to move along the paths that occasionally passed by a cottage. They were relieved that there were no lights on in any of them.

Finally reaching the path that led down to Singing Beach, they almost collapsed with relief when they saw Chap's boat bobbing just off the shore. They half ran, half slid down the rocky embankment to the beach.

Chap was motioning to them to hurry and frantically waving a lantern. If another boat passed by Singing Beach, they would be sure to remember that they saw Chap Harris's boat anchored off shore. Swept by crosscurrents, this was not a spot where any of the locals fished. If the *Land's End* were spotted, there would be questions.

"What will you do when you get to London?" Bess asked.

"I don't know, but something better than what I'd be doing in prison, half a world away." He hugged her awkwardly with one arm. "Thank you, my Bess."

"Here. Here is Chap's key to the prison." Bess pressed it in his hand. "Give it back to him. Oh, Harry," she said. "I don't have any money to give you to help you when you get there."

"I don't want any money from you," Harry protested.

"Just wait. Please wait." She ran over to the rock outcropping.

"I can't, Bess—I have to go." He headed down toward the water. She reached inside the little cave and grasped the bottle with the cross and the slave's note inside. Running after him, she pressed it into his hand.

"Take this. I hid the cross here so Elsie couldn't steal it. It's real gold and pearls—you can sell it once you get to London for some money to tide you over."

"Now!" Chap's rasp came over the black water. "Now, or I'm leavin' without you!"

"What about the note inside?" Harry asked, looking at the bottle.

"Agnes May has been cooped up in that cave long enough. It's high time she set off on another adventure. She'll be fine company for you."

Chap had already started to pull up his anchor, and the water was slapping hard against the boat's hull.

"It's now or never," he called out. "Come on, lad!"

Harry tucked the bottle inside his waistband and waded out to the boat, grabbing the edge and hanging perilously onto the side. For a moment it looked as though the boat had pulled away from him and Harry had been sucked under the inky water. Chap leaned over the side, plunged his hand in, and grabbed Harry's arm. Bess let out a gasp as she watched him yank Harry aboard. She could see he was drenched by the time he was hoisted up on to the *Land's End*, his clothes hanging off his lean frame. It occurred to her then that he had nothing else to wear.

Chap guided the boat carefully out of the cove and into the open channel. She knew Harry would be watching minutes later as the tops of the island houses he'd known all his life vanished into the ghostly clouds.

She stood on the beach, fingering the carved heart in her pocket and watching until the boat had disappeared.

"Take care of yourself, Harry," she said softly.

Bess hoped that when the *Land's End* was close enough that they could see the lights of Portsmouth flicker in the distance, Harry would be able to relax a little. Chap could sail the waters between the island and mainland with his eyes closed and his hands tied behind him. He would drop Harry off, go do his usual fishing and pull in to the dock at the Isle of Wight with his catch just like he did every day. She had no idea what would become of a young boy brought up in the country trying to make it alone in the city. But it was out of her hands now. She hurried to get home before she was missed.

Chapter Thirty-Three

The next morning the talk on the island was about Harry Fletcher's escape from Parkhurst Prison during the night. The small police force, led by Constable Fletcher, searched the entire island and then searched it again. They combed the forests and inquired of the ferry routes to the mainland.

"Do you even know how he escaped?" Elsie demanded of the embarrassed constable when he came to report the incident to her personally. Bess stood quietly behind her stepmother.

"We do not, Your Grace. Perhaps he hid in a supply-delivery cart. We're checking with the suppliers now. But I knew you would want to know directly. I truly don't believe you have anything to fear from Harry."

"I know, I know, Harry is a good boy," she mocked. "Save for the fact that he's robbed us blind and is now on the loose, a desperate prison escapee, no less!"

"We'll find him, ma'am. We always find them," the constable halfheartedly assured her. "No place to go on the island. He'll get hungry sooner or later."

He turned to Bess. "Would you have heard anything from him? I mean, you two being friends and all? Did he say anything when you visited yesterday?"

"No. I have no idea, constable," Bess replied flatly. "Blame an innocent boy for something he hasn't done and put him in prison. There's no telling what he'll do."

"Oh, for heaven's sake." Elsie threw her hands up and rolled her eyes. "Do you see what I have to endure?" she asked Alfie. "Anything, anything at all to defend this thief."

A sad look passed between Alfie and Bess before Bess turned away and walked toward her bedroom.

"I give my word that we'll find him shortly, Your Grace," Alfie said. "And we'll let you know as soon as we do. Put your mind at rest."

Bess heard Elsie sigh heavily as she abruptly closed the door.

From her bedroom window, Bess watched poor old Constable Fletcher hop on his bicycle, his face as red as a plum as he pedaled off down the drive to search for Harry.

~~~~~~~~~~

Two days later, Bess frantically scanned the front page of the *Island County Press* newspaper, which confirmed what islanders had been speculating:

Between the black moonless night and the heavy fog, Chap Harris may never have seen the steamship Annabelle *before it was full upon him, ramming his small boat and slicing it clean in two.*

The captain of the Annabelle *threw life preservers overboard in the hopes that some poor soul might be able to use one. But he told investigators that he doubted it. He reported the accident an hour later, when he pulled into port in Portsmouth.*

Rescue boats searched for hours, but all they found was debris from the smashed boat and one empty life preserver drifting nearby.

~~~~~~~~~~

When there was no word of Chap turning up anywhere, he was first presumed and then, two weeks later, declared dead.

A small memorial service was held on the island. Bess overheard the few fisherman friends of Chap's whispering among themselves about why a duke's daughter was in attendance.

Bess stopped going to the library for a while. She couldn't bear to pass by the dock and see a strange boat in Chap's old mooring. It was clear from island talk that Harry's parents blamed everyone at Attwood Manor for what they publicly insisted were ruinous lies that cost them their only child. They never believed Harry was guilty. They also refused to accept that he had died trying to escape the island. They lit candles weekly in Whippingham Church for their son. But after two months of intensive searching, it was assumed that Harry had either made it off the island or died trying.

No bodies ever turned up. Not Chap's. Not Harry's. After the first few weeks, Bess realized she might never know. But she prayed that maybe the stonemason's son might be safe—perhaps he was somewhere where he could find his own true north.

~~~~~~~~

Three months after the sinking of the *Land's End*, Bess and Sarah were eagerly counting down the weeks until the Duke of Kent would return from Africa. Bess had carefully planned out the conversation she would have with her father when he returned to Attwood. She felt certain that he would believe her. He would have the resources to locate the dealer on Bond Street and verify that it was Elsie, not Harry, who was stealing from Atwood. But there was little she could do without him here.

There had been no word from him in over a month, but in his last letter he wrote that he would be in Zanzibar soon and he still expected to be back on the Isle of Wight by the first of March.

So when a letter with no return address arrived one day for Lady Bess Kent with the postmark too smeared to read, she tore it open expecting to find a note from her father. A single piece of paper with the letter S on the front fell out of the envelope. She flipped the sheet over. On the back it read, "S. For safe."

MARY MARGARET

The bottle was lost in the English Channel when Chap Harris's boat was destroyed. From there, the North Atlantic Drift, a powerful warm ocean current that merges with the Gulf Stream, picked it up. Currents, like giant rivers, move constantly through the world's oceans. Before this was understood, sailors would stop their boats for the night, only to wake up bewildered when they found themselves miles away from where they stopped. Two identical objects released at the same location at the same time, affected by storms and winds, can end up in dramatically different areas.

If the bottle had entered the water a few hours later or a few miles farther out, or if an unexpected storm had struck during its journey—it could have very well ended up in Africa or India or almost anywhere in the world where land touches the sea.

Chapter Thirty-Four
BOSTON, MASSACHUSETTS, NOVEMBER 1856

"When you're done, I'll have you drop off Mrs. Dartmouth's shoes at her house on your way home," Mr. Eaton said, popping his head between the red velvet curtains that divided the ironing and storage area from the front of his shop.

"I'm finishing up now, sir," Mary Margaret answered, placing her hot iron down on its pad to cool. She'd pressed three dozen shoe- and bootlaces, and then threaded them back into their respective shoes. It was usually only two hours' work four days a week, but Mr. Eaton paid her eight pennies a week for it, and there wasn't much else a twelve-year-old Irish girl could do for work in the city of Boston. And besides, Elton Eaton's Boot and Shoe Repair Shop was close to home on Beacon Hill, just four blocks from the basement apartment that Mary Margaret shared with her parents and younger sister.

She didn't mind the work. Unless she peeked out,

she couldn't see the customers from where she labored behind the curtain. To pass the time, she made a game of guessing who they were when they entered the shop—by the sound of footsteps, the scent of cologne, or the dead giveaway of their voices. Some were easy, like Miss Beatty with her musical voice like a flute, or Mr. Finn with his big donkey voice that mismatched his elf-sized feet.

She pulled yesterday's newspaper from the pile that Mr. Eaton had next to his desk in order to wrap Mrs. Dartmouth's shoes, but stopped when she noticed three paragraphs circled in red. The first item was titled "Lonely Hearts Advertisements."

She skipped down and read the second circled paragraph. "Widower, forty-four years of age who does not drink or smoke seeks warmhearted lady for purpose of marriage. Owns small shop with living quarters above. Signed—Boston Shoe Man."

Mr. Eaton must've made the marks on the paper, Mary Margaret realized. Several columns below he had circled: "Upright young lady looking for a warm hearth and a warm heart. Not the least pretension of beauty, but I am patient and gentle and have all my own teeth. Favorite pastimes—reading and correspondence."

"Oh no!" Mr. Eaton reached over and took the

newspaper from Mary Margaret. "Please use tissue paper until I tell you differently. I've been saving the newspapers lately."

"Yes, sir," she said and reached for a sheet of tissue paper. Mr. Eaton was an orderly man. Every morning he read that day's newspaper from cover to cover, and then set it neatly on top of the growing pile. "Are you saving them to kindle the stove fire?" she inquired, wondering if he'd mention the Lonely Hearts ad.

"No," he said, smiling. "For something else— something of a personal nature."

Mr. Eaton is going to get himself a new Mrs. Eaton, Mary Margaret thought excitedly. She decided not to ask any more. Ma constantly warned her to remember her place.

Mary Margaret knew that poor Mr. Eaton had been all alone since his dear wife had passed away three years earlier. They had no children and he had no other relatives. At the end of the day, he closed up his small shop and retired to his apartment on the second floor. Mary Margaret didn't think he spoke a word to another soul until the next day when he came back downstairs. He seemed to enjoy chatting with his customers, and she thought he had come to appreciate her abilities and sense of humor.

"You have common sense, Mary Margaret," he often said to compliment her. "That's a quality that seems to be in dwindling supply."

Mary Margaret took one last look at the tiny back room to be sure she left the iron on its pad and every-thing in order before closing the red drapes behind her. The front of the shop wasn't much bigger than the back room. The shoemaker loved to read and was a student of history. Along with his tools and shoe bench, stacks of books lined the walls, with still more neatly piled on the floor. There were books about how to identify birds by their song, how to recognize a sil-versmith's mark, and by what manufacturer a china platter had been made. And there were dozens more books, many about the faraway places that Mr. Eaton hoped to visit someday. It seemed as if every question Mary Margaret had, Mr. Eaton had a book that held the answer.

"Shall I come back later today, Mr. Eaton?" she asked. "Do you have anything else for me to do?"

"No, no. You can leave for the day. I have company coming soon."

"I noticed that you bought some flowers for your tea table," she said, fishing for more information.

Mr. Eaton laughed. "Very observant. It is a lady I'm expecting. Her name is Daphne Cummings."

"Oh, Mr. Eaton," she cooed. "'Tis a lovely name. She sounds like a beautiful spring flower!"

"Well, we shall see. She is coming over in an hour for tea," he said.

"Does she live close by, sir?" Mary Margaret asked.

"Several blocks from here with her ailing mother, I'm afraid. That's why we haven't met before. Her mother isn't long for this world, and she doesn't want to upset her by bringing around a fellow. So I can't visit her at her home just yet."

Mary Margaret thought about that and said, "I would think her mother would be glad to know that when she left this world her daughter was going to have a fine man like you to keep company with her, if you don't mind me saying so, sir."

Mr. Eaton blushed a little. Then he said, "Well, we'll just have to see. But you'd better be getting off. Mrs. Dartmouth will be looking for her shoes. Go along now."

She tucked Mrs. Dartmouth's shoes under her arm and headed out into a light, wet snow, pulling her frayed coat close around her neck. The crown of her hair, still damp from sweating over the iron, froze in little tufts that stood up like waves.

Reaching the top of the hill, she rapped the brass knocker on the Dartmouths' door. She was getting ready to leave the package inside the front vestibule when a beefy hand grabbed the back of her dress and pulled her backwards into the street.

Chapter Thirty-Five

"And what do we have here? A little mick out stealin' from the good folks of Beacon Hill?" A booming voice split through the cold air.

"Put me down," Mary Margaret hollered, kicking her feet. "I'm not stealing anything!"

"Sure you're not! What do you have there in your hand? Let me see that package," the man demanded. She could see now that her assailant was a police officer with a nasty-looking club hanging from his belt. He put her down, but kept a tight grip on her arm and eyed her with a look of mistrust so true that it took her breath away.

Before Mary Margaret could say another word, the door swung open, and Mrs. Dartmouth rushed out. "Oh, officer! Oh, my goodness. What in heaven's name is going on here?"

"See here what I found? Little Irish riffraff trying to steal this package from you! Caught her red-handed." His face lit up, proud of his catch. Mary

Margaret figured he was hoping the lady would slip him a coin for his troubles.

"Oh, Officer Dyer, no. You've made a mistake. This child works for Elton Eaton. She's *delivering* my shoes, not stealing them!"

Officer Dyer—for that was the name on the brass name tag, Mary Margaret now noticed—looked suddenly deflated.

"An Irish girl?" he asked, incredulous.

"Well, yes. You don't need to be an Englishman to deliver shoes, for heaven's sake," Mrs. Dartmouth replied haughtily. She took the package before disappearing back inside her house.

Mary Margaret looked down at her feet, and Officer Dyer glared at her.

"I'll escort you out of the neighborhood," he finally said. "If you're not doing errands for someone, the likes of you don't belong here."

"But I live in this neighborhood," she said, trying not to sound too defiant.

"Really, now?" His eyebrows rose up. "Well, let's see where, shall we?" Mary Margaret started to walk to her apartment in silence, with Officer Dyer following closely behind, slapping his club against the palm of his hand. The longer he slapped it, the more annoyed she became.

Who does he think he is, the King of England? she thought.

Halfway up the street she stopped in front of a brownstone, turned around, looked him straight in the eye, and said in her most polite voice, "Thank you officer, for escortin' me home."

"Why you . . ." But no sooner had he reached out and sunk his fingers into her arm than a stronger arm pulled him away.

"See here, what are you doing with this girl?" George Bennett was not pleased to see commotion in front of his house as he arrived home from work.

"Da!" Mary Margaret said when she saw her father rushing up behind Mr. Bennett. It was just past five o'clock, and Tomas Casey, Mary Margaret's da, who worked in Mr. Bennett's shipyard, was also returning home.

"This is my daughter, officer," Da sputtered, hiding his balled fists in his pockets.

"See here," Mr. Bennett continued. "What in heaven's name is going on here? Officer? Explain yourself." Mr. Bennett placed himself in front of the policeman, and Mary Margaret rushed into her da's arms.

"Sorry, sir. The girl says she lives here!" Officer Dyer bellowed. "And this fellow now says he's her father.

Some kind of father-daughter swindle for sure. It won't be the first I've seen from the likes of these people."

"They *do* live here. I'm George Bennett. This is my house. The Caseys live below stairs in my home and work for me. Has young Mary Margaret committed some legal offense, sir?"

"You got an Irish family livin' in your home?" the policeman asked, screwing up his red face.

"I do, and what of it?" Mr. Bennett snapped.

"I see. Well." Officer Dyer put his club back in his belt.

"Again I ask you," Mr. Bennett said, clearly agitated, "has the girl committed any offense besides walking in her own neighborhood?"

"Well, no. No, I just assumed . . ." The street in front of the house was growing busier with people returning home from work, and Mr. Bennett didn't like the attention the incident was drawing.

"Well, all right, then," Mr. Bennett said. "Let's break this up and go back about our business. I, for one, am ready for my dinner. Good night. See you in the morning, Tomas." He patted Da on the shoulder and went inside.

Officer Dyer and Da, both breathing heavily, stared at each other for a long moment until finally the policeman hissed under his breath, "Catch the girl so much as spittin' on the sidewalk, and I'll clock her." He gripped his club and gave it a menacing little shake.

Da didn't blink, but Mary Margaret could see his chest heaving under his coat.

"I hear ya, Officer," was all he said between tightly clenched teeth.

"It's all right, Da—he didn't hurt me." Mary Margaret pulled at his sleeve to come inside, shuddering at how tense his body was beneath his jacket.

Chapter Thirty-Six

The next day, Mary Margaret and Louisa Bennett sat on the Bennetts' parlor-room carpet with a large crate of doll clothes, carefully picking through the box and examining each piece. Boots, the Bennetts' cat, stretched out next to them, occasionally flicking her long black tail or licking the white paws she was named for.

"My dolls don't wear this anymore," Louisa announced, holding up a little black wool cape. She put it in the stack she was making to give to Mary Margaret. Mary Margaret's doll had just one cotton dress that her mother, Rose, had made from an old tea cloth. *Now*, she thought, *my doll will have a wardrobe fit for a queen!*

"This one has a little tear in it." Louisa scowled at a blue flowered dress.

"Oh, I don't mind at all. My ma taught me how to sew long ago. I can stitch that up like new," Mary Margaret said, quickly adding it to her growing pile.

As the girls were sorting, Louisa's parents sat with their coffee, watching their only child play.

"George, I've been thinking, and if the President of the United States can have a Christmas tree in the White House this year, then so can we have one here," Mrs. Bennett said to her husband, leaning in closer to him. "The papers say Mrs. Pierce is going to set one up in the East Room and decorate it with holly and pinecones and sprigs of green, and she and the president have invited groups of children to visit and sing 'Hark, the Herald Angels Sing' around the tree."

Mr. Bennett looked over at her, squinting through his wire-rimmed spectacles, and said, "Franklin Pierce won't be president much longer, my dear Aurelia. All his talk against freeing the slaves in the South has cost him the election."

"It would be so festive in our parlor's bow window," Mrs. Bennett mused.

"My dear," Mr. Bennett sputtered. "I want our daughter to know that Christmas is about a great deal more than sitting around a dead tree and eating candy out of an old sock."

She leaned over and rested her hand on his. "Oh, please, George? What harm would it do, dear?"

"Oh, Papa," Louisa piped in. "We could have little

candles and even candies on it. I think it would be so very grand!"

Mrs. Bennett stood up and went over to the window, scooping up Boots and absentmindedly scratching behind the cat's ears. "Of course, I know many people are still dead set against it. They want it to remain a simple, solemn day. Frances Lowe next door feels very strongly about it."

"Frances Lowe hasn't an ounce of good cheer left in her for anything," Mr. Bennett grumbled. "She is against everything fun. Cranky old woman, if you ask me. I tell you, I feel sorry for her students at that girls' school."

"George, be kind." Mrs. Bennett frowned and glanced over at the girls. "Frances is an excellent teacher. Poor dear, since her husband died all she has left are her pupils and her son, Lucas. You know he was only sixteen when he sailed off two years ago to California looking for gold. My word, he was just a boy! Frances is hopeful he'll be back any day, perhaps before Christmas."

"You know what they say, my dear." Mr. Bennett looked up at his beautiful wife. "God doesn't give anyone more than they can handle."

"On the contrary, George," she said with a sigh. "I

see people all the time who have been given more than they can handle."

Mary Margaret's head popped up from sorting doll clothes, and she asked, "Excuse me, but did you say that Lucas Lowe will be home for Christmas?"

Louisa also looked up and said, "Will he, Mama? He's been gone forever."

Mary Margaret and Louisa had tagged after Lucas every chance they'd gotten when he'd lived next door, and had both been crestfallen when he left to go out West.

"I'm not certain, girls. I notice his mother keeps a candle in a lantern in her front window all night now," Mrs. Bennett said, peering at Mrs. Lowe's brick house next door. The drapes were closed tightly except in the bow window, where the lantern shone brightly.

"But I met her coming back from the Custom House the other day," Mrs. Bennett continued, twisting a piece of her dark hair behind her ear. "She was checking to see if there was any news about when ships from San Francisco are due in. Remember when Lucas was a little boy, George? Frances used to take him sledding on the Common, and she would go down the hill on the sled with him. She was the only mother who did that! And she would laugh as loudly as any of the children. I think she just set to worrying when Lucas went out West. She'll feel sunnier when he returns."

"Excuse me, but I need to get home now. My ma will need me to help with supper," Mary Margaret said, carefully packing up her new doll clothes. "Wait till I show all these to Bridget."

"How is your sister, dear?" Mrs. Bennett asked.

"Even more under the weather this past week, I'm afraid," Mary Margaret answered. "But Ma says she thinks she sees the color coming back to her cheeks." She left through the back door, being sure to close it tightly the way her ma had instructed her, and then hurried down the steps to the Caseys' apartment.

The Bennetts had finished the cellar rooms in their Mt. Vernon Street house quite nicely. On the side of the house, an outside staircase led down three steps to a basement apartment where the Caseys lived. At the bottom of the stairs, a door opened directly into their tidy little kitchen with worn floors, a table and chairs, and cast-iron stove set into a hearth. The small clock the Caseys had brought with them from Ireland ticked softly on a mantel above the hearth. Two small bedrooms were off the kitchen, one for Tomas and Rose and one for their daughters, Mary Margaret and her younger sister, Bridget.

Mr. Bennett had a peaked roof built over the cellar's entrance, so the rain wouldn't dash in or the snow fill up the stairwell in winter. Mrs. Bennett had planted a flowering vine that twisted up and over the roof, providing a little shade in the summer and a lovely fragrance when it bloomed every spring.

The Caseys fed the kitchen stove all winter with sea coal from the backyard shed to heat the three rooms, and Ma kept every inch of their tiny home spotless. On the wall behind the table where they took their meals, she hung a picture of the Blessed Virgin Mary.

Like every Irish child, Mary Margaret knew the history of the Great Hunger. She and her family had fled Ireland, along with thousands of their starving countrymen, when the Potato Famine struck. Irishmen in Boston still repeated the sorrowful stories over and over. In 1845, the leaves on potato plants suddenly turned black, curled, and eventually rotted. It was unlike any other crop failure they'd seen before. The working people of Ireland ate meals of boiled potatoes three times a day, but it wasn't long before they went from being hungry to starving.

Mary Margaret was convinced that what little joy Ma had in her died the day two crewmen tossed Mary Margaret's brothers' lifeless bodies overboard in the middle of the Atlantic Ocean. Tad and John weren't the only ones. Ireland's potato famine sent tens of thousands of starving souls on ships bound for the United States. Fleeing on overcrowded, rickety ships, hundreds of exhausted, starving passengers died just like the Casey boys of typhoid and other diseases before they reached America's shores. Mary Margaret knew Ma also blamed herself and the meager diet she had subsisted on while pregnant with Bridget for her sister's frequent illnesses. Lately, there were days when Bridget had been so sick she couldn't leave the bed.

Mary Margaret was proud that when Mr. Bennett needed skilled workers for his growing shipbuilding business, out of thousands of men, Da was chosen. Cheap Irish labor was pouring into Boston, and a friend of Mr. Bennett's who worked at the immigration station kept an eye out for possible workers. It was he who recommended the Casey family. Mr. and Mrs. Bennett met them and felt confident that the couple would be a good fit—Rose as household help and Tomas as a skilled craftsman.

The Bennetts were told the family had lost two sons on the trip over, though Mary Margaret's da never mentioned it to Mr. Bennett. One day when Ma and Mary Margaret were cleaning the Bennetts' first floor parlor, Ma had paused over some of the Bennett family photographs, and her eyes had filled up. Mrs. Bennett had touched Ma's hand and said gently, "I'm so sorry about the loss of your little boys."

Ma's face had softened. "Thank you, ma'am," she said. Mary Margaret had known her ma was grateful for the kindness. "I'm still their mother in my dreams," Ma said.

Chapter Thirty-Seven

The temperature had dropped, and it had snowed still more. By morning the city was covered with a pearly white blanket and the narrow streets were slick with ice. Pedestrians tried their best to steer clear of horse-pulled carriages, since occasionally one of the big beasts would skid, causing its cab to swerve back and forth.

Mary Margaret loved the days when her father would take her downtown with him on errands for the Bennetts. Their breath spilled out in clouds as they made their way down Beacon Hill past the gold-domed State House and the fine houses on Pemberton Square.

Scollay Square was filled with the smells and sounds of horses, street vendors, and sailors fresh off ships. Well-to-do merchants and tradesmen strutted about in black top hats as they came and went from the shops, law offices, and small businesses that catered to the wealthy residents of Pemberton Square.

Mary Margaret and Da's first stop was the Old Corner Bookshop, where they presented the clerk with a list of books that Mrs. Bennett planned to give as presents.

"I'd like to work here someday," Mary Margaret said, marveling at the rows and rows of leather books that lined every wall.

"Growing tired of ironing shoelaces for Mr. Eaton, are you?" Da asked.

"Not really," Mary Margaret answered thoughtfully. "We talk a lot. And he talks to me like a friend, not as though I'm an annoying child. Of course, that might be because he has no one else in the world to talk to except for me and his customers."

"Perhaps you'll even have one of your own books on these shelves someday." Da patted her arm. "You keep writing in your journal. The parts you've shared with me I've much enjoyed. Sure I have."

She looked down at her feet for a moment before she spoke. "I write about all our lives, Da. Some of it is very sad. What little I can remember of our crossing when we lost Tad and Johnny, even. And I write about how Ma still cries for them when she thinks we don't hear her. The one about the boys is called 'The Coffin Ship.' Ma says that's what they called the boats that brought us over because so many people died. But I also write about joy. There is a fair amount of that to be had if you want to find it."

"Choose joy, Mary Margaret," her father agreed. "It is a choice. Always choose joy."

"One of my best stories is about the day Lucas Lowe took Louisa and me sledding."

"Ah, yes." Da brightened. "The one you call 'The Red Sled.' Sure that's your ma's and my favorite of all the stories you've shared with us."

"Lucas Lowe is coming home, you know," she said.

"I heard!" Da replied. "That will be a fine day. He's a good boy—a man now, I imagine."

The bookshop clerk, presenting Da with a bundle neatly tied up in brown paper and string, interrupted them. "Tell Mrs. Bennett that I think she'll enjoy her selections. And wish the Bennetts a Happy Thanksgiving and a Merry Christmas for me."

A small bell above the door tinkled as they left the warm shop and trudged back out into the cold, snowy street. Da lifted his daughter over one particularly slushy puddle.

"Now down to the docks to pick up a fresh fish for the Bennetts' stew tonight," Mary Margaret said.

Long Wharf jutted out farther than any of the others, allowing large ships to tie up and unload directly into the warehouses and shops. The salty air took on a nasty bite as they walked to the end of the dock. Bell buoys clanged in the harbor, and people bustled about doing their errands. Everyone's head was tucked down against the bitter winds. Mary Margaret pulled her coat tight around her and wished she had a warmer scarf.

They purchased two pounds of cod from a fishmonger, and despite the bitter cold, Mary Margaret asked if they could walk along the wharf a bit to look in the windows. A teashop, barbershop, and other shops selling bright-colored threads and toys had begun to decorate their doors with festive greens and berries.

"I don't suppose it will do any harm," Da agreed.

"Louisa told me that the pirate William Fly was executed here," Mary Margaret piped up. "And his body was hung above the wharf for everyone to see!"

"Ah," Da said. "Louisa is a fountain of information."

"She's the one who will be a writer," Mary Margaret said with confidence. "She practices all the time. She's read all the new books. She let me borrow *The Lamplighter*, and I could hardly put it down, Da! Louisa said all her girlfriends want to be just like Gertie. She's the girl in *The Lamplighter*."

"Is that what they teach her in the fancy school she attends?" Da asked.

"That and many other things. She studies etiquette—

that's a fancy word for nice manners—embroidery, painting, music, and how to pour tea and coffee. She practices the tea pouring for me some days. She's wonderful at it.

"She also learned that a lady never shows her ankles." Mary Margaret thought about that for a moment. "But I don't care if anyone sees my ankles or not. I'd rather pick up my skirts than let them drag on the ground and get wet and dirty."

"Very practical of you," said Da.

"If I had the choice, I would rather attend Mrs. Lowe's school," Mary Margaret offered.

Da could barely hide his surprise. "You joke! Old Mrs. Lowe? I doubt she is fond of us Irish, Mary Margaret."

"Yes, I know. But I think she just may have a good heart under her bluster. Lucas is so kind, Da. She couldn't have a son like that and not have some kindness in her heart."

"Aye," Da agreed. "Lucas Lowe was always good to all of us."

"And she teaches important things at that school. Louisa has told me all about it. Things that, between you and me," Mary Margaret said, grinning at Da, "I think are more important than tea and ankles."

Chapter Thirty-Eight

"We need to be getting back," Da said. "I don't like the looks of that sky, and if it snows again tonight, I'll have to be up in the dark to clear the Bennetts' walk and still get to the shipyard on time."

"Oh Da, wait—stop. Down there. Look at that. What is it?" Mary Margaret stopped short, leaned over the wharf, and pointed down into the water at a small object bobbing against the pilings.

"There's a lot of trash floating around the docks, Mary Margaret," Da said. "It's probably what's left of some sailor's evening ale."

"No, it's like a genie bottle. The light is glinting off it. Can you see?" she said.

"Lord, Mary Margaret, your imagination."

"I'm serious, Da. Can you fetch it for me?"

He looked down at the bottle floating along the surface. All manner of things collected around the wharves.

"Ah, Mary Margaret," he groaned. "I don't really

feel like retrieving a dirty old bottle from under the wharf."

"It might have a genie in it—you can't be sure," she said with a twinkle in her eye.

"You don't believe in genies now, do you, lass?" he asked.

"Of course not. But it does look interesting. It looks special. Please, Da?"

"All right, all right," he said. "Let's see if it will come up."

Da borrowed a long pole with a hook at the end from one of the fishmongers and lowered it into the water. The first time he managed to snag the bottle, it fell off the hook. Again, his hook caught and slipped.

"I think, Mary Margaret, that it doesn't want to be caught." He gave it one more try before Mary Margaret knew he would begin insisting they head back home. This time, dripping with saltwater and bits of wharf moss, the hook held. Bringing the bottle up gingerly, Da unhooked it, plucked off the weeds, and presented it to his daughter.

"That won't make much of a stew for you tonight," the monger joked when Da returned the pole.

"Your ma will have my head for letting you bring that smelly old thing home," Da said, frowning.

"I'll clean it up, Da. Can you open it for me? Please. It looks like there is something inside. Some paper and something that makes a little rattle and catches the light."

He pulled his pocketknife out, carved away the wax seal, and carefully wiggled the top up until it gave way, spilling out the contents into the palm of his hand.

First came out an engraved gold cross with tiny pearls embedded in it. There was an empty spot in the middle where one pearl was missing. A rolled-up note had also fallen out. Mary Margaret's eyes lit up. She let out a whistle as she carefully unfolded it and then read aloud:

Agnes May Brewster
Born: July 1843. Colored slave.

Da let out his own low whistle and said, "Well, now, what do you know."

"Can I keep it?" she asked.

"Well, I'm not of a mind to toss it back in the drink after working so hard to get it out. But let's take a closer look at it when we get home. Right now we need to get back."

They hurried home, speculating what the contents

might mean and what the cross might be worth. But first they stopped to drop the fish and books off at the Bennetts' kitchen door.

"Now wait a minute, Tomas." Mrs. Bennett lifted a butcher knife and cut off a big chunk of the fresh fish. "Give this to Rose for your dinner tonight."

"Oh, Mrs. Bennett, I couldn't—" Da said, politely refusing.

"You can and you will. Enjoy your dinner, Mr. Casey. Mary Margaret, I know you like fish stew." She smiled as she closed the door behind her.

When Da and Mary Margaret appeared in their own kitchen, they called Ma and Bridget over to the table so they could show them their newfound treasures. Bridget was still in her nightdress, her face drawn and pale. *At least she's up and out of bed*, Mary Margaret thought.

"I think the cross is real gold, Tomas," Ma said after a moment, her eyes shining. "But what would a colored slave and a gold and pearl necklace be doing in the same place?"

"There are initials on the back of the cross." Mary Margaret squinted and held it up closer to the lantern. "D-S-S, J-K. I think. Aye. That's what they say."

"Dissjik?" Bridget scrunched up her nose, pronouncing the initials as one word.

"No, you squirrel! That's not a word. I think they're initials—the first letters of a person's name," said Mary Margaret. "I just can't imagine whose."

"Sure I don't know. There's no way of telling such a thing," Da mused. "I'm afraid that it's going to remain a mystery. One thing is certain—DSS J. K. does not stand for Agnes May Brewster."

Mary Margaret sat up straight. "Someday soon I could be working in a Lowell mill, maybe even on the same cotton that this Agnes May had picked just months before."

"It's possible," Da said, nodding.

"I can take it with me the next time I go to Mr. Eaton's. He might know something about it. He's a wealth of information, he is," Mary Margaret said. "I can keep the bottle and its contents, right Ma?"

"Aye, put it someplace safe, though," Ma said. "I'd have you return it, but I don't know how you'd go about findin' the owners. We'll find out the value of the cross. We could use the money."

"Oh, Ma, I don't want to sell it," Mary Margaret pleaded. "I want to wear it. I think it must have meant a great deal to someone at one time. I can't imagine why it was tossed out to sea."

"I can't see that would do any harm, Rose," her father said. "At least for now."

"Yes, yes," her mother sighed. "But wash that bottle well so it won't smell up my house."

"I will, Ma, and thank you," Mary Margaret said.

But her mother was already storing the fish Mrs. Bennett had sent down before heading upstairs to prepare the Bennetts' dinner.

Chapter Thirty-Nine

A few days later, Mary Margaret bent over the dark, cherrywood desk that Mr. Bennett had installed in a sunny corner of Louisa's fourth-floor bedroom, and carefully read the articles and letters Louisa had written. Louisa propped up the November issue of *Merry's Museum Magazine* against the back of the desk as she tucked a curl behind her ear. Like her mother, she wore her dark hair pulled back in a bun, except for two long ringlets that hung down in front of each ear. Every month when the illustrated magazine arrived, she devoured its contents. She especially enjoyed that fashions of the season were discussed.

"I send in article after article and get back rejection after rejection." Louisa dropped her head on her desk.

Mary Margaret looked around slowly. She'd never been to the fourth floor. Two enormous rooms faced each other and took up the entire floor, save for a small landing at the top of the stairs. Tall windows looking out onto Mt. Vernon Street were framed with heavily embroidered draperies that complemented a carpet woven with a swirly leaf pattern. A quilt decorated with roses covered Louisa's four-poster bed, and a coal-burning fireplace was on the opposite wall.

On top of a bookcase a dozen china dolls sat lined up by size, each dressed in fine garments trimmed with braid, fringe, cording, and tassels. Over the fireplace hung a framed sampler that read "Home Sweet Home," which Mary Margaret knew Louisa had made herself when practicing her sewing skills.

All Mary Margaret could think was, *Imagine sleeping in a palace like this. I could fit our entire apartment in her bedroom and still have room left over.*

"Inspired by such grand surroundings, Louisa," Mary Margaret gushed, "elegant words must pour from your pen!"

"You would think, wouldn't you?" Louisa laughed. "I wish it were that easy for me."

"Just don't give up," Mary Margaret urged her. "So much of your writing is worthy of being published. Truly it is. This one is my favorite," she said, pulling out the one letter from Louisa's sheaf that mentioned Mary Margaret and her freckles. "I wouldn't have believed my own eyes if my name had actually appeared in a magazine!"

"Well, it didn't." Louisa looked on glumly while Mary Margaret read the rejected letter aloud.

Dear Mr. Merry,

I very much appreciated your short article about people with large feet. I am one of those people. I can tell you from experience that it does not feel good when others laugh at them and pronounce that I could sail across the ocean on them. So it was a pleasure to read that while some people think that large feet are ungenteel for a lady, you think they are convenient because these people have a better chance in a high wind than those with small feet.

I also liked your suggestion that large feet are more convenient for kicking rascals.

My friend Mary Margaret has a great number of freckles on her face. So do her mother and her sister, Bridget. She doesn't like them, but her mother and sister don't seem to mind them at all. Mary Margaret's father told her that an Irish girl's face without freckles is like a sky without stars. So I suppose everyone has something about themselves that they don't like.

Respectfully,
Louisa Bennett, Boston

"Now Louisa, that's clever writing!" Mary Margaret declared after she finished her enthusiastic reading.

"You don't mind that I used your name and discussed your freckles?" Louisa asked.

"Not at all," Mary Margaret said. "My da always says to take no offense where none is intended. I'm only sorry that *Merry's Museum* hasn't seen the quality in your writing yet. Just don't give up. I think perseverance will pay off."

"Pay off indeed," Louisa laughed. "Papa says if I actually get an article published in the magazine he'll give me a silver dollar!"

"Well, now, that *would* be something!" Mary Margaret had never actually held a silver dollar, a fact she kept to herself.

The girls agreed that what Louisa needed was new material to write about.

Mary Margaret had decided not to tell Louisa about the bottle she and Da found. It was going to make the best story in her journal. She felt a little tinge of guilt, but it was too good to share just yet.

Chapter Forty

"And ooohh, the faerie folk. Watch out for them, Louisa." Mary Margaret's blue eyes grew wide. "They have been known to snatch up naughty children from their parents and leave a stranger in their place."

Louisa was sitting at the kitchen table, listening raptly, her teacup suspended in midair. "All these stories, Mary Margaret. Leprechauns and banshees, pookas and changelings. Ireland must be a fearsome place."

"Not if you know your way around," Mary Margaret boasted. "And if you're careful to watch out."

Ma hummed softly to herself while she put the finishing touches on the Bennetts' dinner, and Mary Margaret washed and dried the dishes and pots while regaling Louisa with her stories.

"Was Bridget asleep when you checked in on her?" Ma asked.

"No, she was reading her primer in bed," Mary Margaret answered. "She seems a bit perkier today, Ma."

"Let's hope," her mother answered. But Mary

Margaret noticed Ma's forehead was pleated with worry lines.

Ma often told her daughters that she didn't mind cleaning and cooking in the Bennetts' sunny kitchen with the sounds of the dishes and pots clattering, the smell of food baking or roasting. She had confided that the last few years they had lived in Ireland she woke up every day worrying how she would put food on the table. Bare cupboards. Empty potato bins. Barren fields blackened with scarcely a turnip to dice for a watery stew. They'd begun to live off wild blackberries, nettles, old cabbage leaves, edible seaweed, roots, green grass, and even roadside weeds. Mary Margaret had vague memories of that time.

After those days, Ma often told Mary Margaret and Bridget, she would never take the smell of supper cooking for granted.

"You could be the writer, Mary Margaret," Louisa said. "The stories you tell are wonderful. And if you write them down half as well as you tell them, you should become an author, too." Louisa drained her cup with a slurp. A drop fell on the flounce of her skirt, and she brushed it off absentmindedly.

"No, I must work for a living as soon as I'm able. But I do write in my journal a lot. Stories about my life," Mary Margaret said. "Sometimes about the customers that come in to Mr. Eaton's. I wrote a story about the time Lucas Lowe took you and me sledding on the Common, and that strange man asked him if I was an Irish mick, and Lucas threatened to sock him in the nose if he called me a name again!"

"Ha! Wasn't he wonderful that day?" Louisa said. "He was so brave. Oh, Mary Margaret, won't you let me read your journal?"

She was flattered to think that Louisa, living in this grand home, with her beautiful dresses and fancy rooms, would want to read what she wrote.

"Mary Margaret, it's time to go," her mother announced, placing a cloth over the still-hot bread and a cover on the beef stew she'd prepared for the Bennetts' dinner. "Did you fill the scuttles with coal from the back?"

"Yes, Ma," she answered.

"Well, then, pick up your wild stories and your coat and say your thank-yous for the tea and cookies."

"Mary Margaret, I have a thought," Louisa said. "Can you run down and get your journal now? I can begin reading it tonight, and you can come back for tea when I'm done, and we can discuss it. Oh, please? Your stories are too dear for me to wait another day."

They both looked at Mary Margaret's mother.

"Aye. You can run along now and fetch it," her mother said, slipping her white apron over her head and tucking it in the wash hamper.

"Louisa," Mrs. Bennett called down to the kitchen. "Please change for dinner."

"Just bring it up to my bedroom," Louisa said. Before vanishing up the staircase, she wrapped two fresh cookies in a napkin and gave them to Mary Margaret. "Here, these are for Bridget. Please tell her I'll be glad when she feels well enough to come back upstairs with you and your mother."

It wasn't hard to locate her journal in their little home. The Caseys had so few possessions that everything was easy to find. Her father said that was the wonderful thing about how they lived now: no one had to hunt around through a lot of useless clutter for their belongings.

Ma said that when Da, the eternal optimist, died, she was going to have an old Chinese proverb carved on his tombstone. It would read: *Now that my house has burned down, I have a better view of the mountains.* He often hopefully referred to Bridget's symptoms as growing pains, which irritated Ma to no end. "Joint pain, numbness, too weak some days to even walk?" Ma would sputter. "Tomas, I don't know what it is—but I know what it isn't."

Ma brewed endless teas and herbal poultices, all recipes from the old country, that she packed on to Bridget's swollen knees and ankles in a vain attempt to make her youngest child robust again. At times they seemed to help, but then Bridget would take another turn downward.

Out of breath from running down the stairs and back up, Mary Margaret was anxious to take another look around Louisa's bedroom. Days when she helped her ma with chores at the Bennetts', she often watched as Louisa rushed up the stairs after school with her friends. They all dressed alike, with long bell-shaped skirts decorated with laces and braid. Sometimes they would bring their dolls along—even they were dressed in finery such that Mary Margaret could not have dreamed of.

"It's all right, dear. Just go on up." Mrs. Bennett waved her toward the stairs. Mary Margaret walked her best ladylike walk past the third floor where the Bennetts' bedroom was, making sure to keep her eyes downcast.

"Louisa?" she called out softly when she reached the top of the staircase.

"In here," Louisa called from her room, as she finished adjusting the bow on the back of her dress. Mary Margaret placed her journal in Louisa's hands as if it were a precious jewel.

"I swear, I will take care of the beautiful prose in your journal like you can't imagine. You have my solemn oath on that," Louisa vowed.

"I know you will. We'll discuss it another day, perhaps over tea, like you said." Mary Margaret Casey tossed her shawl around her neck with a flourish and marched back down to her home.

Chapter Forty-One

Mr. Eaton was bent over a pair of black patent-leather slippers, his balding head shining in the light, when Mary Margaret came to work early.

"Well, you are eager to get to your ironing today!" Mr. Eaton said, glancing up at the clock.

"Yes, sir," she said. "But I was hoping you might have a minute to look at something my da and I pulled up from the docks the other day. Sure it's a grand mystery, Mr. Eaton."

"Well, it's slowed down a bit here, so I don't suppose it would do any harm. And I do love a good mystery. What is it you have there? Let's have a look."

She pulled the bottle from the bag where she had carefully stowed it and placed it in his hands.

"Mr. Eaton, sir, there is a note that appears to be about a slave's birth and a splendid gold cross on a chain inside. My ma says it would fetch a pretty penny."

"Oh, my." He carefully shook out the note and cross before pushing his spectacles up on his nose to get a better look. He squinted and held the bottle and gold cross closer to the light.

"The bottle certainly has an unusually wide mouth on it," he noted. Then he rubbed his finger over the bottom. "Here. Here is a marking. See this? It's an anchor. Looks like an anchor inside a circle." He explained to her that some things could be told about bottles by their markings, and perhaps the bottle she found had such identifications. He moved his head so Mary Margaret could see for herself, and she leaned in and examined it.

"What would that stand for?" she asked.

"Let me see," he said, rifling through a few different stacks of books. He pulled out a thin volume about glassmakers and their identifying marks from one of his tallest piles. He thumbed through carefully for several minutes until he stopped and slapped a page. "Aha! Look here!"

Together they studied a page that had a drawing of the anchor inside a circle, exactly like the one on the bottom of her bottle.

"What do you suppose it stands for?" she asked.

"Well, let's see. It says that it is the mark on bottles that were made at the Richmond Glass Company in Richmond, Virginia. Of course, we can only speculate how or where it went into the water. The bottle could have been made in Virginia and ended up anywhere after that. That's really all that we can know from this."

"The cross looks to be real gold." He rolled it over in his fingers. "DSS J. K.," he read. "Doesn't mean anything to me. They appear to be someone's initials."

Mr. Eaton examined the note that was inside the bottle. "Perhaps a slave girl on a Virginia plantation. Again, no way of really knowing, I'm afraid. You were right about one thing, Mary Margaret—it is a grand mystery, indeed!"

He carefully returned the note and necklace to the bottle and handed it back to Mary Margaret. The bell above the door tinkled and a customer entered, inquiring after her boots.

Chapter Forty-Two

The next week Mary Margaret arrived at Mr. Eaton's shop bubbling over with curiosity about Miss Daphne Cummings. Mr. Eaton hadn't mentioned her again, but Mary Margaret now noticed the smell of cinnamon whenever she came in to work. None of their regular customers smelled of cinnamon.

"Good morning, Mary Margaret," Mr. Eaton said.

"Good morning, sir." She gave him a sly smile, and he returned it.

"How is Miss Cummings, if you don't mind my asking, sir?" she said, hoping she wasn't being too bold.

"Well," he began, "Miss Cummings has visited here two weeks in a row now. She's a very fine lady. And I met her this morning for a walk by the Frog Pond. I'll see her again this evening, as well." He looked down at his lap and blushed. "And every evening after that she's free and will see me."

"And I believe she smells of cinnamon." Mary Margaret tilted her freckled nose up.

"She does indeed." He chuckled. "But of course, we can only see one another for a couple of hours a few times a week because of her mother. Apparently, Mrs. Cummings is terribly ill. And poor Daphne is all the family she has in the world. The dear girl is limited as to what work she can do, as she needs a cane to get around. I don't want to be indelicate and ask her what she uses it for, but it seems she has a slight limp."

"Ah. I understand. My sister sometimes needs a cane and it does slow her down, but she still manages quite well. Da says that sooner or later everyone has something they must learn to live with.

"Well, then," Mary Margaret continued. "As I see it, sir, you and Miss Cummings are both practically alone in the world. So it's a grand thing that you've found one another."

"It's true," Mr. Eaton said. Mary Margaret hoped he wasn't feeling embarrassed at having shared so much. "Well, now, enough of this idle chatter. If we don't get to our work, I won't have money to pay you or to take my new lady friend out for tea and cakes!"

Chapter Forty-Three

Mr. Eaton barely looked up when Mary Margaret reported for work again the next day. She immediately saw why. There were at least twice as many shoes and boots as usual waiting to be repaired and cleaned.

"I've left three dozen pair out there for you. You'll have your work cut out for you this morning," Mr. Eaton said. "Seems with the holidays that everyone wants to look their best."

The scent of cinnamon lingered in the air, and she spied two empty teacups on a tray by the stairs. *Looks like there's going to be a new Mrs. Eaton*, she thought gleefully as she disappeared behind the red drapes.

They each worked in silence for the next hour, knowing that at noontime, the customers would come flocking in on their lunch break looking for their footwear.

An hour and a half into their work, the bell above the front door tinkled. Mary Margaret heard a customer enter and let out a sob.

"Miss Cummings!" Mr. Eaton jumped up from his bench, wiping his hands. Mary Margaret stopped ironing and stood quietly peering out from the small opening where the curtains met.

"Oh, Mr. Eaton." She heard the lady's voice breaking. "I had nowhere else to go. No one else to go to. I'm sorry."

"Sit down, sit down," he said. "Is it your mother? Has she taken a turn?"

"No, no. It's, it's . . ." Daphne, looking pale and weak, leaned on a dainty white cane in one hand and clutched a handkerchief in the other.

"Tell me," he urged. "And here, please sit down. Now, there, there. Tell me, what is it?"

"Well, Mother has needed more and more medicine to keep her comfortable in these final months," Daphne explained between sobs.

"Of course." Mr. Eaton patted her hands. Mary Margaret could see that she was a tiny woman, with little birdlike features and pale brown hair twisted up in a bun. A bright red hat with a jutting feather was fastened at a slight angle on top of her head. She had a pleasant if rather unremarkable face, except for very large dark brown eyes.

"And because she is bedridden, she is cold all the

time. So sometimes I have purchased extra coal for the fires," Daphne whimpered.

"Naturally." Mr. Eaton nodded sympathetically.

"Between the medicine and the coal and the doctor's bills . . . oh dear. I'm so ashamed. The rent is two months past due, and I do not have the money to pay the landlord. He's threatened to throw Mother and me out on the street!"

"Daphne, Daphne. Is that all?" He sat back and visibly relaxed. "I thought there was a problem we couldn't fix. We can take care of this."

Mr. Eaton took a key from a chipped cup on the desk against the side wall and opened the bottom drawer. He lifted out a metal box, opened it, and pulled out a small stack of bills.

"What do you need to bring your accounts up-to-date?" he asked firmly.

"Elton, I will pay you back—I give you my word. It might take me a month or two, but you'll get back every cent." She swiped at her tears with her gloves, and he handed her a fresh handkerchief.

"I know you will," Mr. Eaton said.

Mary Margaret couldn't make out the amount Daphne asked for, since the poor woman was still weeping, but she saw Mr. Eaton peel off several bills from the stack and watched as the lady tucked them neatly in the reticule she carried.

"Dry your eyes and go take care of your obligations, my dear. I will see you tonight." He stood up, passed her the cane, and helped her to the door.

After she left, Mr. Eaton pulled the red drape open and looked down at Mary Margaret. "I ask you," he said, "to please not repeat what you just heard here."

She nodded gravely. "I promise, Mr. Eaton. I won't say a word."

Chapter Forty-Four

Mary Margaret struggled to keep up with Louisa as she rushed down the street and up the steps of the Boston Girls' School. Her feet had grown that fall, and her shoes pinched her toes. There was no use complaining, as she already knew there would be no money for new boots or shoes until next year. Louisa's hands were tucked inside her fur muff to keep them warm, so Mary Margaret pulled back the brass knocker and rapped several times. The door swung open, and Mrs. Lowe stood looking down at the two of them. She was dressed in a stiff blue dress with a skirt shaped like a church bell, and the mourning broach she'd worn since her husband's death was pinned tightly at her collar.

"Yes?" she asked.

"Mrs. Lowe," Louisa said breathlessly, pulling a hand from her muff. She held up the letter her mother had asked her to deliver. "This letter was mistakenly delivered to our house instead of yours. Mother says it looks like it's from California and that I was to bring it directly to you."

The older woman's face took on a light that Mary Margaret hadn't expected from Mrs. Lowe. It touched her heart. Mrs. Lowe took the letter and opened the door wide.

"Come in Louisa, dear. You, too." She nodded at Mary Margaret. "You'll freeze out here. Hyacinth!" she called out. A young woman appeared from around the corner. "Please give the girls some tea or hot chocolate and show them around. Then deliver them to my classroom to wait for me." She spun on her heel, carefully opening the letter as she disappeared into her office.

"Would you like to have a tour of the school?" Hyacinth asked.

"Oh, yes. I go to the Young Ladies' School on Beacon Street, and I've heard of this school. A friend of mine is a student here," Louisa explained. "She says it's awfully hard, and she must study even on weekends. I'm not sure that would suit me."

The blue and purple multipaned glass windows poured light like a rainbow on tall rows of bookcases that lined the walls. There were three large, sunny teaching rooms on the second floor, and Mrs. Lowe's and Hyacinth's offices were on the first floor. One classroom had twelve desks lined up neatly in three rows of four. The other rooms had chairs placed evenly around a long oak table. A box in the center of each table held several freshly sharpened pencils.

"Do you study needlepoint here?" Louisa asked.

"No," Hyacinth said. "Our girls study the classics, mathematics, science, history, and some study the French language."

"I would love to study all those things," Mary Margaret said.

"My father says that young ladies need to be educated so they can make fine wives and mothers," Louisa said. "I don't see how mathematics and science can help with that."

"Sit here, ladies, and I'll bring in cups of hot chocolate," the teacher said over her shoulder as she disappeared below stairs to the cellar kitchen.

Mrs. Lowe appeared at the same time as the hot chocolate, and Mary Margaret thought she looked as though she had been crying.

"Is everything all right with Lucas, Mrs. Lowe?" Mary Margaret asked.

"Yes." She smiled. "He should be home by Christmas. Oh my goodness, what a sight for sore eyes he will be."

"What else does he say, Mrs. Lowe?" Louisa asked. "Has he discovered gold?"

"Well, he doesn't say, so I'm not sure. But he's having fascinating experiences." She thought for a moment. "Would you be interested in hearing his letter?"

"Oh, yes!" Mary Margaret cried, forgetting herself.

"Please, oh yes, please," Louisa agreed.

Mrs. Lowe took a deep breath and began to read slowly:

Dear Mother,

Pick out the fattest Christmas goose at the market; I am coming home at last! Please forgive the long absence since you last heard from me. I hope this photograph of your handsome son will make up for it a bit. There are photographers camped out here with simple, portable cameras who will take portraits for twenty-five cents. Don't fret if I look a little gaunt, I'll quickly gain back the weight when I return to Boston and your splendid cooking.

Perhaps you have read in the newspapers that the gold fields here are almost picked clean. After just five years, the gold rush is all but over. Fortunes have indeed been made by a lucky few, but more people have made money selling to the miners than the miners have made prospecting for gold. Picks, shovels, food, shelter, and all means of required supplies are wildly overpriced. Of course, once one is here, what are we to do? There is nowhere else to buy these necessities.

The talk is growing here that there may be a war if the Southern states try to secede and if they do not free the slaves. Can this be? At first I thought it was just foolish gossip, but now everyone who arrives from the East says it is so. How can it be that after all we went through to become a free nation, we would now turn on each other?

I have booked passage on the schooner Liberty, *departing from San Francisco and arriving in Boston mid- to late December, depending on the seas and the weather.*

I have so much more to tell you, Mother.

Your devoted son,
Lucas

Chapter Forty-Five

Together they scanned every detail of Lucas in the photograph he'd enclosed. He did look thinner. His hair and sideburns were a little scruffy.

"The barber down in Pemberton Square will tidy him up." Mrs. Lowe kissed the tip of her finger and touched it to the picture. "If he really makes it home before Christmas, we'll go to church together, and then I'll roast a wonderful goose for dinner."

"Oh, Mrs. Lowe. I can't wait to see him," Mary Margaret spoke up.

Mrs. Lowe tucked the letter tenderly in her skirt pocket. "He's been in California all this time, so it will take a while for his blood to thicken up and get used to our New England winter. I've almost finished knitting a pair of mittens for him. Red with thirty-one white stars around the cuffs—fifteen on one mitten, sixteen on the other. Lucas will know right away they represent the thirty-one states in the union, and thus the stars on the American flag. We Lowes are nothing if we're not patriots!" she finished proudly.

"Does he still have the drawings that Mary Margaret and I did for him before he left?" Louisa asked.

"Why, yes, Louisa," she laughed. "And I haven't changed a thing in his room, except to tidy it up after he left. His bookcase still holds his books—*Aesop's Fables*, biographies of great men the likes of Marcus Aurelius, and another favorite, *The Journal of Lewis and Clark to the Mouth of the Columbia River* by Meriwether Lewis. I guess those stories of adventurers inspired him and fired his imagination.

"And your drawings are hanging above his dresser. The one you drew, Louisa, of skating on the Frog Pond. And the other, Mary Margaret, of all three of you flying down Boston Common on a red sled.

"Your drawings and his favorite quote from the Roman emperor Marcus Aurelius are the only things he hung up."

"I remember him quoting that to me," Mary Margaret said.

"He wrote it out and framed it," Mrs. Lowe said. "I've looked at it so many times that I know it by heart." She clasped her hands on her chest and recited: "'Do not act as if you had ten thousand years to throw away. Death stands at your elbow. Be good for something, while you live and it is in your power.'"

It was more than either girl had ever heard Mrs. Lowe talk about anything, and they both fell silent, not wanting her to stop.

"Oh my, where are my manners?" Mrs. Lowe suddenly said. "I'm just going on and on. Did you enjoy the tour of the school?"

"Very much, ma'am. I am wondering, do you teach the girls here to write stories?" Mary Margaret asked, unable to hide her enthusiasm.

"Why, yes, we do. Aren't you clever to ask? We teach history and math in the morning. After lunch the girls pull out their required journals and share their writings. When you see me sitting in my window by the lamp at night, I am often correcting their journals for them. I hope to produce some talented writers from our little school. We finish up the afternoon with science, spelling, and penmanship. Once a week we study geography and current events."

"I love to read and write, but I have a headache just thinking about the rest," Louisa laughed. "We'd better be on our way. Mary Margaret's mother is making us a pot roast for dinner, and I can almost smell it from here."

"Thank you, girls." Mrs. Lowe dug into her pocket and pulled out a penny for each of them. Mary Margaret almost took it, but Louisa demurred, and so she reluctantly did the same. The thought of a bag of tasty candy ran through her mind as well as how long she had to stand over a hot iron pressing shoelaces to earn a penny.

Chapter Forty-Six

"Mr. Merry says we should write about things that we know." Louisa pulled her heavy wool cape up against the morning chill and tucked her dark hair primly under her velvet bonnet. "I think if we wander around a bit, I will find inspiration and something just wonderful to write about."

Mary Margaret was grateful to have a day outside, walking around Boston Common.

"I'm sure you'll make a fine writer someday, Louisa," Mary Margaret enthused.

"I long to be. It's all I've ever wanted to be when I grow up. Some people think it's unladylike for women to be authors, but I think that's terribly old-fashioned. *The Lamplighter* was written by a woman, and it was quite good, didn't you think?"

"I certainly agree," Mary Margaret said.

They walked along, kicking at a snowbank here and there while waiting for the perfect story to come along and plant itself in Louisa's imagination. Mary Margaret again considered telling her about the bottle, but decided to wait longer still. She had begun writing about it and could already tell that it was going to be a grand story, one that was hers alone. Louisa could find other stories to write.

"I like to write, too," Mary Margaret explained. "Mostly in my journal. Someday I would like to learn proper spelling and grammar and maybe even calculating."

"Perhaps you could enroll in school," Louisa said. "There are no Irish children in my school, but I'm sure someplace would take you."

"No. Now that I've finished up with public grammar school, my days of schooling are over. Ma says most high schools cost one hundred dollars a year per pupil. Aye, I'll be getting out to earn a living within a couple of years. Probably in Lowell. Lots of lasses like myself are moving there to work in the mills. Da says that there are respectable boardinghouses for the girls to live in there."

"I'll miss you, Mary Margaret," Louisa said earnestly.

"I'll be home for visits, I think at Christmastime. Perhaps I'll have saved enough money to come with gifts." Mary Margaret smiled at the thought.

"You're very clever," Louisa said. "You'll do just

fine. I'm so inspired reading your stories in your journal. Thank you for letting me keep it all this time."

Mary Margaret beamed and said, "That's all right. Since I have filled the one you have, I have another one I write in. Which stories are your favorites so far?"

"I couldn't pick just one," Louisa said. "I'm halfway finished and honestly, I love so many of them. You have a way with words that is all your own."

They walked toward the bottom of Beacon Street, past the row of stately town houses. The brick sidewalks were slippery and had heaved in the frost, so they rose and fell as if they'd been set by a drunken bricklayer. A pair of dappled gray horses huffed and snorted as they pulled a shiny carriage up the hill, while two stray dogs nipped at their hooves. The driver, wearing a tall black beaver hat, snapped his leather whip at the spotted dogs, yelling, "Here, here! Get away from here!" But the dogs were having too much fun on this cold, sunny day and ignored him.

Children's voices squealed as they raced down the hills of Boston Common on red sleds, scarves flapping behind them, the glimmering State House dome rising in the background.

At the foot of Beacon Hill they turned onto Charles Street, and Louisa waved her gloved hand, pointing toward the swampy Back Bay. "Now here is a story that I think will interest people."

"A smelly marsh?" Mary Margaret asked.

"No. Papa tells me that they're going to bring in tons and tons of dirt from west of Boston and fill in this whole area. You see all that muck? He says lovely houses will stand on this very spot in a few more years. I think people will want to know about this." She smiled, warming to the idea for her writing project. "I think I'll get an article in *Merry's Museum*," Louisa said, beaming, "and my silver dollar!"

Mary Margaret had stopped listening. Her attention had been drawn to the back of a woman wearing a bright red hat with a feather and walking briskly ahead of them down Charles Street.

"What is it, Mary Margaret?" Louisa asked. Mary Margaret had begun to walk in the woman's direction, as if in a trance.

"Mary Margaret," Louisa asked again. "What is it? Do you know that lady?"

Suddenly the woman stopped at the corner next to a tall burly man with scruffy brown hair, and they wrapped their arms around each other and kissed.

"In public, no less!" Louisa scoffed, not understanding what was going on.

When the couple turned and went on their way, arm in arm, Mary Margaret continued to follow them at a safe distance, dragging Louisa with her.

"Mary Margaret," Louisa said. "You're scaring me. What is it?"

"I know that woman. I've been sworn to secrecy, but I can see I'm going to have to tell you. Come on, though, keep up with me." They followed at a discreet distance while Mary Margaret filled her stunned friend in about Daphne Cummings.

"Oh, Mary Margaret, these people might be criminals! And I don't like this part of town. I don't think we should be here," Louisa said. "What if she spots you?"

"She doesn't know who I am. She's never laid eyes on me. And she doesn't know I know who she is," Mary Margaret explained.

Finally, the couple stopped in front of a run-down brownstone rooming house, and the man pulled out a key.

Mary Margaret rushed up to the couple and tapped Daphne on the arm, leaving Louisa standing alone and looking frightened on the corner.

"Excuse me, ma'am?" she asked.

The man turned and looked down at her. He had a

nose that had obviously been broken on several occasions, and he was missing a couple of teeth.

"What do you want?" he asked. "We don't give no money to beggars."

"I'm not a beggar, sir. And I'm sorry to bother you," Mary Margaret said to the woman in the red hat. "But are you Miss Malloy?"

"No," she snapped in a voice that didn't sound anything like the sweet voice she used with Mr. Eaton.

"Well, I was told to deliver a message to Miss Malloy at this address, and they said she was a fine-lookin' lady who usually wore a red hat," she lied.

Daphne patted her hat and smiled a little, "Well, I *am* a fine-lookin' lady, but I am not Miss Malloy. And no Miss Malloy lives in this building."

"See here," the man broke in gruffly, "she ain't no *Miss*. She's my wife. Now like she said, you got the wrong person, so scram."

The couple shuffled into their front vestibule and slammed the door in Mary Margaret's face.

"Poor Mr. Eaton," Mary Margaret kept saying as the two girls made their way back up Beacon Hill.

Chapter Forty-Seven

"But you don't work today," Ma said the next morning as Mary Margaret carefully placed the bottle with the cross and torn page in a small bag and picked up her coat.

"I know that, but I thought if Mr. Eaton took another look at the bottle he might think of something else. He knows an awful lot about many things, Ma."

"You're keeping the necklace inside the bottle?" Ma asked, her eyebrow arching.

"I am," Mary Margaret answered. "I thought on it and decided that Agnes May put it there for a reason, Ma. It seems only right that I keep it safe there for her."

"Well, I guess you have a point." Ma smiled weakly. Mary Margaret knew her mother was tired from another long night. She had been up and down many times with Bridget. Her sister had been complaining more and more lately about the gnawing pain in her hips, and she seemed to have even less strength than usual in her arms. This morning when she tried to sip her tea, it dribbled, and Bridget admitted that she had begun to experience numbness around her mouth.

"Can I do anything to help with Bridg, Ma?" Mary Margaret asked.

"No. She's finally gone to sleep. Go ahead off to see Mr. Eaton. Let's just keep it quiet here so she can rest."

Mary Margaret put on her coat, pulled her scarf up over her head, stepped out into the frosty air, and closed the door softly behind her.

She had gone over and over in her mind how she could tell Mr. Eaton what she had discovered about Daphne. Nothing seemed right. At last she had decided to trust that the right words would come. She didn't really think he would have discovered any new information about the bottle, but it was as good an excuse as any to appear for a visit. She knew she couldn't let him go on not knowing the truth. And she needed to get to him before he gave Daphne Cummings any more of his money.

A sign hung on the door of the shoe shop that said PROPRIETOR WILL BE BACK SOON. The door was unlocked, and Mary Margaret went in to wait. She was wondering how much more of Mr. Eaton's hard-earned money the woman had managed to steal from him when she looked up and saw the red hat with the feather bobbing along outside the shop window. Leaping to her feet, Mary Margaret disappeared behind the velvet drape just as Daphne and her husband entered the shop.

"He keeps it in here," Daphne said. Mary Margaret heard them cross the room and open the desk drawer.

"Ah, the key. He keeps it in this dirty old chipped cup with the faded roses on it." Daphne laughed. "He says that his wife used to drink her tea from it every day. Oh, boo hoo!"

Mary Margaret's blood would have boiled if her heart weren't pounding in her throat. She steadied herself, remembering how mean Daphne's husband had looked. She was just as afraid of Mr. Eaton returning and stumbling onto the scene as she was of being discovered. Since she had approached them in front of their rooming house, they would be sure to recognize her.

"Just take the whole box, Fred," Daphne ordered. "And let's get out of here before he gets back!"

Her husband whistled when he saw the pile of cash inside.

"Is there anything else worth taking in this place?" he asked, scanning the room.

"No, no," she said nervously. "Come on. Let's go."

"I just want to be sure that I'm not leaving behind a nice watch or something else that I might pawn," he said, crossing to the back of the shop, so close that Mary Margaret could smell his hair pomade.

When he yanked back the red drape, his mouth flew open at the sight of Mary Margaret standing on a chair, her arms raised high above her head, clutching her bottle in both hands. She wasted no time swinging it down with all her might across the side of his head. Stunned, he spun back as Mary Margaret jumped off the chair, flew past him, and ran toward the door.

"You!" Daphne's eyes widened as she recognized Mary Margaret, and she jumped in front of the door, grabbing Mary Margaret's arm as Fred recovered his balance.

"It's the girl from the other day! The one who asked us if I was Miss Malloy!" Daphne said, holding Mary Margaret's arm in a vise grip.

"You ain't no delivery girl," Daphne spit out.

"And you ain't no cripple!" Mary Margaret spit back as Fred grabbed Mary Margaret by her other arm.

Just then, the front door flew open, hitting Daphne and knocking her to the floor. Officer Dyer, two other Boston policemen, and Mr. Eaton rushed inside.

"Frederick and Daphne Cummings, you are under arrest!" Officer Dyer shouted, grabbing Fred by the arm and yanking Daphne to her feet.

"Elton!" Daphne's entire demeanor had suddenly changed, and she fluttered her large brown eyes at Mr. Eaton.

"They say there's no fool like an old fool." Mr. Eaton looked sadly at Daphne. "Well, you certainly found an old fool in me." Instead of taking her outstretched hand, he went over to Mary Margaret and lifted her up from the floor where she had fallen during the scuffle.

"Mary Margaret, are you hurt?" he asked.

"No, no I'm fine. I came to warn you, sir. This woman is not who she said she is."

"So I was told," Mr. Eaton said. "Officer Dyer came and filled me in last night. Seems I've been taken, but that's all right. My pride may be even more wounded than my bank account."

~~~~~~~~~

The Caseys' little kitchen was soon crowded with the three policemen, all four of the Caseys, and Mr. Eaton.

"How could you not tell us, Mary Margaret?" Her mother fumed. "Were you out of your mind, lass?"

"I'm afraid it's me you should be angry with, Mrs.

Casey," Mr. Eaton spoke up. "I was a little embarrassed about beginning to keep company with a lady, and I didn't know if it would turn out in marriage or not. I didn't want people gossiping about me. You know how people can be."

"Ah, I do." Ma nodded. "But still, Mary Margaret!" She shook her head and tossed up her hands.

"Well, I can assure you *she* is in no trouble," Officer Dyer piped in. "We had been onto this Cummings couple for a while now. They've been fleecing men with their lonely-hearts swindle around Boston, and some of the gentlemen had come to us to complain. So when I saw Daphne coming and going from Mr. Eaton's shop, I said to myself, 'Well, here she goes again!' And this time we pinned her and that no-good husband of hers. Your Mary Margaret just happened to be there when it all came crashing down. We had informed Mr. Eaton of it just yesterday. He told Daphne he would be out all morning, and we hoped she might come by. That's been their usual pattern in the past. We were right. We just hadn't planned on Mary Margaret showing up.

"And by the way, that was quite the blow ya landed on the side of his head, Mary Margaret," Officer Dyer said, obviously impressed. "What did you hit him with, a shoe hammer?"

Mary Margaret smiled broadly. Then with great drama and flair, she slowly pulled her bottle, miraculously unharmed and with the torn page and gold cross still inside, from her bag and held it up triumphantly.

"'Tis covered in glory, it is!" Mary Margaret declared as she beamed.

Chapter Forty-Eight

Da was already home when Mary Margaret raced down the icy steps to their apartment a couple of nights later. Something wasn't right—she could tell from the looks on her parents' faces. Sitting across from each other at the small table, Ma kept fingering a piece of paper—smoothing it out with her index fingers and tapping it with her thumb.

"What's that? What's going on?" Mary Margaret unwound her scarf and stuffed it up the sleeve of her coat before hanging it on a hook by the door.

Ma didn't say *take your boots off before you come in and get dirt all over my kitchen floor* the way she always did. She just continued to stare at the table and the piece of paper.

"A fella I work with," Da began, "has a daughter with the same problems that our Bridget has. Numbness around her mouth, pain in her hips . . ."

"She knows the symptoms, Tomas, no need for you to recite them," Ma snapped.

"They took her to this doctor. They gave me his

name and address." Da pointed at the paper in Ma's hands. "Doctor seemed to know right away what was wrong. Gave them some medicine that she takes twice a day, every day—a month later, she's as good as new. Almost as good as new."

"And?" Mary Margaret went over and took the empty seat between her parents. "So why the glum faces? 'Tis wonderful news, isn't it?"

Da dragged his fingers through his hair a couple of times and cleared his throat.

She figured out the answer in their silence. "How much does it cost to see this doctor and get the medicine?" she asked, knowing that whatever the answer was, it was going to be too much.

"Where is Bridget?" Mary Margaret then asked, lowering her voice. Ma nodded to the closed bedroom door.

"Perhaps if he met us—" Mary Margaret said hopefully, "this doctor."

"Don't, lass," her mother said. "No doctor is going to see no Irishman without seeing the money first."

Mary Margaret stood up and lifted her bottle from its place of glory on the mantel and carefully shook out the gold cross. "Mr. Hamilton's pawnshop is right next to Mr. Eaton's shoe store. Ma, you said yourself it would fetch a pretty penny."

"Aye, it might," her ma said, brightening a bit. "I

was thinking about selling the clock we brought with us from Ireland."

"There's no need to do that, Ma. The clock was your ma's. I don't need the cross anymore. I wondered why I'd found it, and now I know."

"I'll take it down tomorrow and see what the fellow at the pawnshop says," Da added.

"I'll go with you, Da, on my way to work. Mr. Eaton has asked me to come in the morning. I can introduce you to Mr. Hamilton. He seems nice enough."

"Get washed up, then." Ma stood up, indicating that the matter was settled. "And see if Bridget feels well enough to come out for supper."

Da reached over and wrapped Mary Margaret in his arms, kissed the top of her head, and rocked her a little. "So you see how funny a thing fate is, Mary Margaret? It may turn out that you finding that bottle was indeed meant to be. Ah, lass," he said tenderly, "you have a beautiful heart. That's not something you can put in a child. You were born with it, sure as rain."

∿∿∿∿∿∿∿

Mary Margaret was surprised when she left work the next evening to see the gold cross prominently displayed in Mr. Hamilton's pawnshop window. She had thought it would be gone right after Da brought it down, snatched up within a few hours of being displayed. Mr. Hamilton saw her standing outside and leaned out his front door.

"It won't be here long. Someone will see how lovely it is." He smiled before closing the door against the bitter cold.

Chapter Forty-Nine

Mrs. Bennett gave Ma the morning off to take Bridget to the doctor. Ma, Bridget, and Mary Margaret were the first ones to arrive at his office and the last patients he saw before lunch.

"We were here first," Mary Margaret whispered to her mother when one patient after another was seen ahead of them.

"Hush, you'll get us thrown out," Ma whispered back. "We're lucky he agreed to see us at all. As it is, we had to pay up front."

"Ah. Ah," the doctor uttered when he finally examined Bridget. Ma carefully explained all her daughter's symptoms while he poked and prodded and peered into her ears and eyes and down her throat.

"Well, I think I can help you," he pronounced. "I'm not promising anything, but it looks like a kidney issue that I have seen before."

Ma couldn't help it—she let out a gasp of relief. Embarrassed, her hand flew up to cover her mouth.

"We aren't sure exactly why, but these symptoms seem to indicate a problem with her kidneys not working properly. Leaves too much acid in the blood," he explained.

"If I'm correct, the child needs to take sodium bicarbonate or potassium citrate to correct it. I've seen cases like hers clear up in as little as a month. She's had it untreated for so long that she may have a few lasting complications. She might not grow as tall as she would have otherwise—but nothing that would stop her from leading a normal life."

"That's all?" Mary Margaret asked, incredulous.

"Count your blessings that some problems are easily solved. I'm quite sure this is one of them," the doctor said firmly, scowling at her.

As an afterthought he asked, "I don't suppose either of you have read *A Christmas Carol* by Charles Dickens? Do you know how to read?"

Highly insulted, Mary Margaret spoke up, "We do indeed, doctor. And I have certainly read and enjoyed Mr. Dickens's *A Christmas Carol*."

"I see," he said, a little surprised. "Well, then, you'll remember Tiny Tim and his ailments. A lot of doctors, me included, think that the character of Tiny Tim had a renal disease. That's what I think young Bridget here has. Looks awfully bad and is indeed if untreated. But it's one of those conditions that can be fairly easily addressed. Too bad you didn't bring her in to see me sooner. She might always have a lingering limp. Hard to say, exactly."

They left the doctor and headed directly to the prescription pharmacy on Charles Street. They passed Mr. Eaton's Shoe Shop, and Mary Margaret waved. At Mr. Hamilton's window she felt her heart fall a little when she saw that the gold cross was gone, even though she knew the money was important to her family, especially Bridget. She hoped that whoever bought it would think it was as special as she did.

"Ma, may I go in and see Mr. Hamilton while you get the medicine?" The pharmacy was down only three doors, and Ma was in such fine spirits that she would agree to anything.

"Good afternoon, Mr. Hamilton," Mary Margaret called out, carefully closely the door behind her.

"Ah, I'm guessing you noticed your cross is gone? Yes. Fellow came in just before I closed last night. Never saw anyone so excited. Held it for the longest time, turning it over and over and saying he couldn't believe it. I think he wanted it for his mother. Gave me half the price then and there and is coming back this afternoon with the rest," he said, pulling the cross out from a drawer. "I'm keeping it here until he comes back."

"Was he a fancy gentleman?" Mary Margaret asked. She imagined her cross hanging from the neck of one of the society women who lived on Beacon Hill.

"No. No, in fact he looked to be a common man. A little scruffy, truth be told. Said he works the docks some days. Sounds like he takes whatever work he can get. But his money's as good as anyone else's."

He hesitated for a minute before he spoke very kindly. "I'm sorry you had to sell it, Mary Margaret. I can tell it means a great deal to you."

"I'm content with it, Mr. Hamilton," she said. "It's served its purpose. It was good for something, while it was in its power."

He cocked his head to the side. "Where have I heard that before?"

"Marcus Aurelius, sir," she said. "He said we shouldn't live as if we had ten thousand years, but we should be good for something now, while it was in our power."

"Yes, that's right. It's been a while since I've heard it. It's a fine way to look at life."

He put the cross back in the drawer when the bell over his door tinkled and a customer entered.

Mary Margaret left quietly when Mr. Hamilton approached the new customer, and she rushed up Charles Street to catch up with Ma and Bridget.

Chapter Fifty

The weather had held up until most Bostonians were home from Christmas Eve church services, but soon after dark, a soft snow began to fall and cover the city in a silvery blanket.

"Ah, here they are," Mr. Bennett said as he threw open the front door, thrusting his hand out to Tomas Casey and his family, who stamped their shoes in the vestibule before entering. Da carried Bridget on his shoulders, and she hung on to him with her arms wrapped around his neck.

"Easy, Bridget," he said, "you're near choking your poor old da."

"Oh, my!" Mary Margaret sang out when she saw the tree with lots of candles lighting it up. "'Tis the most beautiful tree I have ever seen."

The Bennetts' tree was splendid, dripping with hard candies and trinkets, its branches aglow with little white candles. The fireplace sizzled and snapped with the sea coal Mary Margaret had carried in earlier in the day.

"Oh, Mary Margaret," Bridget exclaimed, feeling a little superior from her high perch, "you've never seen any Christmas tree before!"

"Merry Christmas, Louisa." Mary Margaret smiled at her friend. Louisa was dressed in a long, black velvet dress with a cream-colored ribbon at her waist, to match the one tying up her dark curls.

"Merry Christmas to you," Louisa replied, not quite looking Mary Margaret in the eye. Instead she scooped up Boots and buried her face in the cat's silky black fur.

"Merry Christmas to you, sir," Da said, pulling off his cap. "And to you as well, ma'am." He nodded politely to Mrs. Bennett. They stood awkwardly for a moment in the front hall, not sure if they had been invited to make a brief appearance at their employers' home, or if they should come in. Mrs. Bennett put an arm around Mary Margaret and steered her to the glowing tree.

"Come right in for a minute." Mr. Bennett waved toward the tree-lit parlor. Mary Margaret noticed that Da didn't take a seat, but stood with his family respectfully at attention. "My goodness, what a week your family has had, Tomas! Rose told us all about the trouble at poor Elton Eaton's shop—and little Mary Margaret being caught up in the middle of it. Thank heavens they caught the scoundrels, and especially that Mary Margaret is fine. You're a heroine, young lady!" Mr. Bennett beamed at her.

This is going to be a lovely Christmas, Mary Margaret thought.

The dining room was directly across the hall from the parlor, and Mary Margaret noticed her mother glance in, admiring the work they'd done together earlier that day. Mary Margaret had polished the buffet serving tables and all the chairs that morning with lemon oil. The long, oval dining table was covered with a freshly washed and pressed damask cloth. She had rubbed the silver candelabras until she could see her reflection, and then Ma had placed them in the middle of the table with candles ready to be lit for the Bennetts' Christmas Eve dinner of goose and plum pudding.

Mrs. Bennett reached up to the tree, pearl earbobs the shape of teardrops fluttering from her ears. "Well, look what I found. A little something for Mary Margaret and another for Bridget."

She placed a bundle of four pencils and a lined notebook in Mary Margaret's hand and a soft blue scarf in Bridget's, each tied with a long red ribbon.

Ma nudged her daughters and they responded politely, saying, "Thank you, ma'am."

"Well, don't untie them now. Save them for your

own celebration," said Mrs. Bennett. "We just wanted to give you a little something for the good service you have given us. We're happy you're with us."

"How lovely your tree is, ma'am," Ma said. "All the ornaments and wee candles. Sure, it's magical."

"Thank you, dear," Mrs. Bennett said. "Some of them we've had for many years. Some are brand-new. This is the first year we've had a tree to show them off, though. George finally consented. After all, if the President of the United States can have a Christmas tree in the White House, the Bennetts can have one in Boston.

"We're particularly proud of the newest decoration for our tree." She plucked a silver dollar off a branch and held it out for the Caseys to see. "Our Louisa has finally had a piece accepted in *Merry's Museum Magazine*."

Louisa shrank farther back into the room, almost disappearing into the potted plants and flocked wall-paper.

"Now, now, come up here, Louisa." Mr. Bennett waved his beefy hand toward her. "Don't be shy. I bet Mary Margaret will be pleased to see she and Lucas Lowe are both part of the story. The publisher sent us an advance copy since Louisa had an article printed. Gosh!" He beamed. "I think it's awfully good."

He picked up the copy of the latest edition of *Merry's Museum Magazine* and pointed to the story.

THE RED SLED
by Louisa Bennett

Mary Margaret edged up to the magazine and blinked hard when she read the title. The first sentence was as familiar as the back of her own hand, and she quickly skimmed over the page. She couldn't believe her eyes. Her words, her story, word-for-word from her journal, but with Louisa Bennett listed as the author. Her parents read the first few lines at the same time, both quickly recognizing Mary Margaret's story.

"Well, you should be proud indeed," Da said, passing the magazine back to Mr. Bennett.

Mary Margaret stared at Louisa.

"How could you?" she barely whispered.

"What's that you say?" Mr. Bennett asked.

"Aw, she's just impressed with your daughter's clever writing." Da clenched Mary Margaret's arm.

"And Rose and I, we want to thank you for your kindness and your gifts. I know the girls will enjoy them. We won't be taking up any more of your time tonight. We'll be going back downstairs. Come on, girls. Rose." Mary Margaret glared at Louisa, ignoring her mother's fierce stare and Da's viselike grip.

Mary Margaret barely heard the large front door with the lion's-head knocker shut behind them, nor felt her feet on the icy walk. It wasn't until they reached their rooms down the little side steps that she burst into tears.

"That beast. She's a beast!" she howled, throwing her bundle of pencils on the floor. "And I want my journal back—now I know why she's had it so long!"

Ma quickly retrieved the pencils. She knew Mary Margaret would need them, and there was no money in the Casey budget for pencils. What the Caseys could not bear was to be tossed out in the street over a story in a magazine.

"We have a roof over our heads, Mary Margaret. Look around you, girl." Her mother's voice was stern. "The Irish are sleeping in sheds and alleys and abandoned buildings. You'll say nothing about this to Louisa."

Mary Margaret nodded but pulled up her scarf and stomped back outside in the icy cold night to sulk on the stoop. Her father followed her, stopping the door from slamming.

"Is this seat taken, Mary Margaret?" Da stood over

his older daughter as she sat shivering in the cold, and draped her coat over her thin shoulders.

"She stole it from me, Da! She stole my story about Lucas and me. How could she? Why didn't you let me say something?"

"You know why," he spoke firmly. "We need this home and this work. The Bennetts are good folks. You must understand, Mary Margaret, if they decide they don't want us anymore, we have nowhere to go.

"Look, she only took from you the words, lassie. She cannot really steal your story. It is yours. No one can take it away from you. And no one can steal your talent either. It is God-given, sure it is."

"I think she's just jealous." She stared up at him.

"I think you're right," he said. "But remember, this is but one story, Mary Margaret. Louisa may never be able to write one as good as this one. But you, you can go on to write hundreds more of them for the rest of your life—stories that will move people. Maybe the story you wrote about our Tad and Johnny. Their lives and their deaths might touch people enough so they can see the tragedy our people are living, and be grateful for what they have, rather than fearing so much what we might take. Tad's and Johnny's lives could have meaning—a wider meaning than to just our family."

She reached up and began fiddling with a piece of the dried vine that hung down off the building, twisting it between her small fingers. Beacon Hill's knotted cobblestone streets lay quiet under the piles of drifting snow. Up and down the street, the candles on adorned Christmas trees shimmered in bow windows.

Da plucked two pods off the shriveled wisteria vine, popped them open with his thumbnail, and stuck one on each of his daughter's ears. He leaned back and smiled at her delicate figure sitting quietly now in the cold silvery evening.

"They should be diamonds," he said.

Chapter Fifty-One

"Hear ye! Hear ye! TER-RI-BLE NEWS!"

The town crier's bell jangled, his long horn clasped tightly to his lips, as he strutted around Scollay Square. Da and Mary Margaret were coming back from the fishmonger's with a pound of cod for the Bennetts' dinner, and like several other people, stopped to listen to the crier.

"Hear ye! Hear ye! The schooner *Liberty* crashed off Lovells Island last night, and all souls have been lost." People rushed out of their shops and up the street as the crier nailed the notice with the list of passengers on the tavern door.

"Da!" Mary Margaret grabbed his arm to steady herself. "Lucas Lowe is returning on the *Liberty*!"

Just then, Mary Margaret saw Mr. Bennett exit a building nearby. He was one of the first to reach the list, and he scanned it quickly.

"It's Mr. Bennett, Da," Mary Margaret said. "He's looking at the posted list of passengers."

Mr. Bennett turned away from the list and the crowd and saw Da and Mary Margaret. He shook his head sadly. That's all they needed. They knew. Together all three rushed up Beacon Hill.

On the way Mr. Bennett gasped and said, "Aurelia told me that she sees people every day who are given more than they can handle. I'm not sure Frances Lowe can handle this."

At the very same time Mary Margaret, Da, and Mr. Bennett arrived home, a messenger from the Custom House whom Mrs. Lowe had paid to keep an eye out for the *Liberty*'s arrival approached her house. She was outside with her cape wrapped tightly around her, sweeping the latest snowfall from her walk.

Mr. Bennett burst through his front door with Da and Mary Margaret behind him, and shouted, "Aurelia! Aurelia! Come quickly. I have dreadful news. The ship Lucas Lowe was on crashed and sank last night. No one survived!"

Mrs. Bennett and Mary Margaret's mother had been peering out the kitchen window at Mrs. Lowe talking with the messenger, and they made room for Mary Margaret, Mr. Bennett, and Da. A dread silence rose among the group as they watched the messenger speak to Mrs. Lowe, his head bowed. He passed her a copy of the notice.

Mrs. Lowe swayed for a second and then slumped to the ground, sinking into her skirt as though she'd been shot through the heart. Mary Margaret watched through the window as Mrs. Lowe sat there on the frozen ground, casting the same shadow as always. But Mary Margaret knew Mrs. Lowe was different now. She would be different forever, just like Ma after she lost Tad and Johnny.

Without a word, Mrs. Bennett and Ma rushed out the door, coatless into the frigid air, and knelt next to Mrs. Lowe, wrapping their arms around her. Mr. Bennett, Mary Margaret, and Da dashed out behind them.

"Tomas," Mr. Bennett said. "Go fetch Doctor Wiggins. Tell him to come immediately. Oh my Lord, tell him Frances Lowe has lost her boy."

Mary Margaret gently patted Mrs. Lowe's back, then dropped her head and sobbed into her hands.

～～～～～～～～

For the next two days, the storm continued to pummel Boston and what was left of the *Liberty*. The tossing sea swallowed up most of the ship and its doomed passengers. On the third day, bodies and debris began to wash up around the city and near the docks. Mary Margaret heard her father tell Ma that three boats had sailed out to salvage what they could, plucking suitcases and floating bodies out of the water for most of the day. When they found Lucas Lowe, he was facedown, fully dressed with full pockets, but the water had pulled off his shoes, and his stocking feet had come up first when they fished his body out.

After being identified, his body was delivered to his mother. Ma told Mary Margaret that he would be laid out in Mrs. Lowe's parlor for two days before he was taken away to be buried next to his father in the springtime when the ground had thawed.

The Bennetts helped her with the burial arrangements. The Caseys didn't need to be told that it wouldn't be appropriate for Irish Catholics to attend the service. Ma baked tea breads and wrapped them in warm towels and had Mary Margaret deliver them to Mrs. Lowe's back door.

"In Ireland, laying out a corpse is woman's work," Ma told Mary Margaret. "When someone passes, we open all the doors and windows to let out any lingering evil spirits and cover up the mirrors to hide the dead person's image.

"We scrub and tidy up the corpse for the wake, then be careful to tie together the departed's hands and their two big toes to keep them from returning as ghosts. And we all carry around a pinch of salt in our pocket to ward off any evil spirits that might be hanging about hoping to steal the dead person's soul."

"Poor Lucas!" Mary Margaret cried. "Should we tell them they need to do all that for him? Mrs. Lowe surely wouldn't want any evil spirits hanging around her Lucas."

"No, no. Don't say anything," Ma said. "They have their own curious ways of doing things here. Not that I agree with them." She sighed. "But still, they have their own ways."

Da made sure Mrs. Lowe's walkway and steps were clear of snow and ice, and Mary Margaret took over a prayer card, and a little note written in her own hand, saying she was sorry for Mrs. Lowe's loss and that she would include Lucas in her prayers every night. She went back to work at Mr. Eaton's and made sure that she always greeted him with a cheery hello. But when she was alone, behind the velvet curtain, she couldn't help crying some days as she ironed. Louisa was so distraught to lose Lucas that she stayed home from school for two days. While Ma kept her thoughts to herself, Mary Margaret knew she was thinking of Lucas, too, since she found a few grains of salt sprinkled in her pocket every day.

Chapter Fifty-Two

Less than a week later, Mary Margaret was helping Ma clean up the Bennetts' first-floor rooms. As she gathered up a pile of newspapers next to Mr. Bennett's chair to discard them, she saw an article on the front page.

The Boston Examiner
December 30, 1856

This winter is turning out to be one of the most severe ever seen in Massachusetts. During the night of the twenty-third a particularly violent snowstorm extended over most of New England, sweeping through Massachusetts with fierce, piercing winds. A church steeple in New Bedford blew down, and there were reports of trees falling across houses. But the gale was particularly disastrous at sea. Several ships were grounded, driven into surrounding rocks and shores.

The schooner Liberty, *so close to its destination,*

hung on through most of the night until the main sail, encased in ice, snapped in the wind and came crashing down, tearing the canvas sail to shreds. From then on it is assumed the hapless ship drifted across Massachusetts Bay and was tossed helplessly by the violent winds, finally driven into the shoal off the northwest end of Lovells Island, tearing out her bottom. Once grounded, the foaming sea must have rushed over the sinking ship, sweeping passengers overboard.

Any survivors would have drowned as the vessel smashed into pieces against the rocks. Any cries for help would have been lost in the howling gales, as the last of the passengers would have disappeared beneath the cold, black water.

She couldn't bring herself to throw it out. Instead, she carefully folded it, and when she went back home, she tucked it into one of her old journals.

~~~~~~~~~~

Mary Margaret appeared from the apartment carefully carrying a steaming cup of tea and waited on the sidewalk while her Da sipped it. She looked up at Mrs. Lowe in her window watching Da bent over, working.

She had lost track of how many times he had quietly gone in the early morning to remove the snow from Mrs. Lowe's walk.

Mrs. Lowe came outside carrying the red mittens with the white stars around the cuffs that she had told Mary Margaret and Louisa she had knit for her Lucas. She put them in Da's hands.

I knew she had good in her, Mary Margaret thought.

"Aw, Mrs. Lowe," he protested. "I don't expect anything. Sure I can't."

"You can. Please, Mr. Casey. My Lucas would want his gloves keeping a good man's hands warm, not sitting useless in the parlor." She turned and disappeared back into her home. Mary Margaret was sure that somehow, Lucas knew his mother was "being good for something, while it was in her power."

Chapter Fifty-Three

The first week in January, early in the morning, Mary Margaret found an envelope addressed to her on the floor just inside the door to the Caseys' apartment. Inside was a letter.

Dear Mary Margaret,

Please accept the enclosed silver dollar that Papa gave to me for having a story published in Merry's Museum Magazine. I have no right to it, and it is burning a hole in my conscience as surely as if it were a hot coal. It is your story of the day we spent with Lucas and his brave defense of you. He was a fine boy, and I know your heart aches as mine does at the thought of never seeing him again. It is your story, as is the splendid talent you have for telling a tale that spellbinds the reader. If you don't mind, I would like to keep your journal for a few more days. I am almost finished reading it, and it has given me more pleasure than I can say.

Please forgive me for what I did. I have learned my lesson from this unfortunate event that I brought upon myself. I have confessed to my parents who are woefully disappointed in me. They agree that this silver dollar belongs to you.

Sincerely,

Louisa

P. S. If you can come for tea someday soon, I'll show you all the latest things I have learned at school. I hope you'll come.

Mary Margaret had already forgiven Louisa. After Lucas Lowe was killed, one magazine article didn't seem so important anymore. Although she did want her journal back, her parents had forbidden her from mentioning so much as one word about it.

When Mary Margaret showed the letter and silver dollar to her parents, her father said, "'Tis good to forgive your enemies, and even better to forgive your friends."

Her mother agreed, but—always the practical one—added, "Good to know we have a spare dollar. We might be needing it."

"What will we use it for, Ma?" Bridget asked.

"I don't know yet. But there is always something

that we need. The money we got for the cross won't last forever. When it runs out, this will buy more medicine for you, if you still need it. But both Da and I think you already seem quite a bit better," Ma replied hopefully. "Don't you agree?"

"Yes, Ma," Bridget said, exasperated. "I keep telling you and Da that I feel better every day but you still keep asking me."

Her mother laughed. "I guess Da and I just can't hear it enough, that's all." She fluffed the back of Bridget's hair and made a funny face at her.

"Help me start supper, Mary Margaret," her mother said.

Ma cut turnips and potatoes into chunks and slid them into a big pot while Mary Margaret peeled carrots.

"Mary Margaret!" Ma cried. "You're going to peel those carrots down to nothing. What's wrong with you?"

She stopped peeling and began instead to chop them.

"I said, what's wrong with you?" Ma put her knife down and turned to her daughter.

"It just doesn't seem fair," Mary Margaret finally said.

"What are you talkin' about?" Ma asked.

"For the price of a doctor's visit and some pills, Bridget could have been better a long time ago. If

Louisa had been sick, don't you know the Bennetts would have had her at the finest doctor in Boston straight off. It's wrong, Ma. And what about people who don't happen to find a gold cross floating by the docks?" she said mockingly. Tears streaked down her cheeks. "Well, I guess they just won't get well, aye? It just doesn't seem fair, that's all."

"Oh, I see," Da piped up from the table. "It's fair you want. Well, life is not fair. No one ever told you it would be."

"Quickest way to break your heart," Ma said quietly, wiping her daughter's tears with the edge of her apron, "is to think life is going to be fair. Don't waste your time complaining about it. Take my word for it, it won't change a thing."

Chapter Fifty-Four

"How many hours do you work today?" Ma asked Mary Margaret the next morning as her daughter pulled on her coat and wrapped her thin scarf around her head, tucking it neatly into her coat.

"I'm not sure, Ma," she snapped, still too angry to look at her parents. "We don't have as much work this week. Seems everyone wanted their shoes and boots spiffed up for the holiday. It's quieted down a bit now."

"Well, if you have the chance, stop in and thank Mr. Hamilton again for advancing us the money on the cross before he'd sold it. He didn't have to do that. You were right—he is a fine man."

Mary Margaret didn't have to be reminded to check in with Mr. Hamilton. She was curious to learn if the man had come back with the rest of the money.

She stopped before opening the door to leave and still staring straight ahead, said, "I'm not angry at you, Ma. I don't know who to be angry with. I just know some things are not right."

"There are a lot of things in this world that aren't

right, lassie," Ma said softly. "You'll either learn to live with that truth, or life will break your heart."

Mary Margaret was relieved to see that Mr. Hamilton's Pawn and Jewelry Repair Shop was open when she arrived a few minutes early to work.

"Ah, Mary Margaret! Do you have any other treasures to sell today?" Mr. Hamilton greeted her when she entered.

"No, sir. My ma wanted me to stop in and thank you again for giving us the money before you even knew if you could sell the cross."

"Oh, I was sure I would eventually sell such a lovely piece. And sell it I did!"

"The fellow came back, then?" Mary asked, lighting up.

"He did indeed. Just about to close up when he came rushing in counting out the money and asking me if I could send it out for him. Said he didn't have a return address, and if it got lost or damaged he wanted to be sure it would come back."

"No return address?" Mary Margaret asked.

"Not so surprising," Mr. Hamilton said. "The city is becoming filled with a lot of temporary workers, and they rest their heads at night wherever they can. I was happy to do it. He paid me extra to send it off for him and to enclose a note.

"I've been busy and haven't sent it yet, but I have everything right here." He reached under the counter and pulled out a box neatly wrapped in brown paper with the address written on it.

Mary Margaret examined the carefully printed address and wished she could open it and read the note, but she knew Mr. Hamilton would never allow it. The address read:

Lady Bess Kent
Attwood Manor
Isle of Wight, Great Britain

"A lady, Mr. Hamilton! Do you think she lives in a castle?" Mary Margaret asked.

"I wouldn't know," he said, chuckling. "The note he asked me to include made it clear that the necklace is important to this Lady Bess, though."

Mary Margaret looked at him, amazed.

"I thought you'd feel better about selling it," he said, "if you knew it was off to someone who seems to hold it so dear."

"Oh yes, I do," she said softly. "Is the fellow who bought it a young man?"

"Yes, fairly so. Looks to have had a bit of a hard life, though. His hands were rough and calloused.

Looks like he might have been a fine-looking fellow if he'd had it a bit easier, if you know what I mean."

"That I do," she said, folding her own hands, red and chapped from the cold and the iron's steam. "Did you get his name?"

"No, no. I didn't ask, and he didn't seem to be in any hurry to offer it. And he paid in cash, so there's no way to trace him."

Chapter Fifty-Five

Mary Margaret hummed an old Irish tune she'd learned from her da, rolling the silver dollar over and over between her fingers before dropping it into the bottle with the piece of paper about Agnes May Brewster's birth. Such an adventure this little bottle must have had. If only it could speak! She wondered what it would be like if she were tiny enough to slip into the bottle and be cast out on the ocean currents to who-knows-where. She imagined a story about a magic bottle that could talk if a secret phrase was spoken. *Ah! That will be part of the next story I'll write*, she thought.

Too much cluttered her thoughts to sleep well at night. She worried about poor Mrs. Lowe. Streaks of white had suddenly begun sprouting in her hair almost overnight. And Mary Margaret had dreams about the mysterious Lady Bess. At first she dreamed she was an old dowager dripping with royal jewels. Lately she had become a princess, held captive like Rapunzel.

From the windows high on the walls in their base-ment apartment, Ma and Mary Margaret watched the feet and legs of people walking past. They recognized the tiny boots of Mrs. Bennett and the long, black shiny dress of Mrs. Lowe as the two ladies carefully picked their way down the Caseys' icy steps and rapped on the door.

"Heavens," Ma said, twisting her apron between her fingers. "Whatever could they want?" Except for the day they moved in, none of the Bennetts had ever been down to the Caseys' rooms.

"I can't imagine why they would be coming here." Ma glanced around the room as if looking for some-thing to pick up or to put in order, but they owned so little that nothing was out of place.

Ma opened the door, and Mary Margaret saw her ma's face flush at the sight of the beautifully dressed women standing at her doorstep.

"May we come in, Rose dear?" Mrs. Bennett touched her arm gently.

"Of course, of course. Shall I put on some water for tea?" Ma asked nervously.

Mary Margaret realized that Mrs. Lowe was carry-ing the journal that she had lent to Louisa. She couldn't imagine why Louisa would have given it to

Mrs. Lowe, and she tried to remember if she had written anything that could get her into trouble. Why else would these ladies come to the Caseys'?

"Oh, no, we won't take up that much of your time. Is Tomas here?" Mrs. Bennett asked.

As if on cue, Da came trudging down the steps, stamping the snow from his boots before he came in. Ma would have his head if he dragged in snow and dirt.

Mary Margaret saw that he was as surprised as Ma to see the two ladies standing in the little kitchen, and he quickly pulled off his cap.

"Tomas—good evening," Mrs. Bennett began. "I have some good news that I would like to tell you and see what you and Rose and Mary Margaret think of it."

"May I?" Mrs. Lowe began. "I hope you won't be offended, Mary Margaret, but Louisa brought me your journal to read. She said you are a gifted writer."

"I hope you don't mind that she did that," Mrs. Bennett interrupted.

"So," Mrs. Lowe continued. "I must tell you that I heartily agree with Louisa's assessment. And Mary Margaret, the story you wrote about the day you and Louisa went sledding with my Lucas . . ." Her chin trembled, and she struggled to continue. "It touched me more than I can say. You have indeed captured my son's kind heart. I treasure that story. And my goodness, it's a rare thing for a young person to write so movingly and with such luminous prose."

Mary Margaret held her head high and made a mental note to look up the word *luminous*.

"Aurelia tells me that you are to go off to Lowell, perhaps as early as next year, to work in the mills there," Mrs. Lowe said. "I have something quite different to propose."

"The mills are a fine opportunity for her," Ma spoke up. "The girls there make good money. She can't be ironing shoelaces for Mr. Eaton forever."

"I won't mind going to Lowell," Mary Margaret said without much enthusiasm. "I hear it's quite exciting there."

"Rose, Mary Margaret," Mrs. Bennett said, leaning forward. "Forgive my frankness. But I must say it. They're only hiring Irish girls now because the American girls have been leaving the mills in flocks. It's hard for me to say this, but you must know the truth. The air in the mills is filled with cotton lint. It floats in the air like snow and destroys the girls' lungs. Many have become ill from consumption."

Mrs. Lowe picked up where she left off. "Lowell aside, I hope you'll consider the proposal I'm about to make. Each year the Boston Girls' School provides one deserving young lady with a full scholarship. It is only for one year, mind you."

No one in the room could miss Mary Margaret's gasp as she fell back against the fireplace mantel. "Me?"

"This year we would like to award it to you, Mary Margaret," Mrs. Lowe said. All eyes turned to the girl who stood thunderstruck against the hearth.

"I assure you, this is a serious offer," she added.

Da scratched his head, "Well, 'tis a very generous offer. We appreciate it. But, we *had* planned on Mary Margaret getting out and working to help out. I just don't—"

"Perhaps the child could help tidy up the class-rooms in the afternoons to help pay for any extras, if that is giving you hesitation," Mrs. Lowe suggested.

"I'd still have plenty of time to keep working for Mr. Eaton," Mary Margaret added quickly. "And Bridget seems to be coming along so well with the new medicine, Ma won't need me as much to look after her."

Rose looked at her husband. Mary Margaret looked at them both. She knew that in their hearts, they no more wanted to send her to Lowell than she wanted to go.

"I can think of nothing in the world I would love

more than to go to school," Mary Margaret spoke up. "Nothing," she added softly.

"The school provides all the books. The only thing Mary Margaret would need to purchase is a school uniform. All our girls must wear uniforms." She passed Ma a piece of paper. "Here is the name and address where it can be purchased."

Mary Margaret squirmed in the silence that followed. But she was determined not to lose this opportunity. She reached up and took the bottle from where it rested on the mantel—covered in glory—and shook out the silver dollar. She looked between Ma and Da, and when she saw the accepting looks on their faces, she held it out to Mrs. Lowe.

"Will this cover the cost of the uniform, ma'am?" she asked.

"Indeed it will," Mrs. Lowe assured her.

"Do you need a moment alone to discuss the offer?" Mrs. Lowe asked as she looked back and forth between Ma and Da.

"I, I don't think that's necessary," Ma said. "Do you, Tomas?"

"No, not at all," Da answered. "A uniform, eh? Well, Mary Margaret, I think you'll look very smart heading off to school in a uniform."

"Don't forget, you'll still have to help me around here with the chores," Ma said quickly, wiping her eyes with the tea towel she had been wringing.

"I won't forget, Ma," Mary Margaret said. "Thank you. I won't forget." She had a lot more to say, but she was afraid that if she tried, she would burst into tears.

"Then is it settled?" Mrs. Lowe asked.

The Caseys looked from one to the other, and Ma spoke up, "Aye, then. It's settled."

Chapter Fifty-Six

It was still dark the next morning when Mary Margaret stole quietly out of bed, so as not to wake Bridget, pulled on her coat, and tiptoed out into the kitchen. The bottle, now considered the Casey family's lucky bottle, rested securely in its place of honor on the mantel next to the clock they'd carried over from Ireland. Agnes May Brewster's birth note was still folded safely inside. Sticking her feet in her father's boots that stood by the door, Mary Margaret crept outside into the dawning light to sit on the stoop—her favorite thinking spot. The wind had stopped, and it seemed as if the whole earth was still. The snow had blanketed everything with a fresh clean coat, and her breath left delicate clouds that trailed off in the clear air.

I'm going to be a student! She thought about how she would march off to school every day in her uniform and learn about writing and science and the great history and adventures of the world. She would have her journey in the classroom instead of in a magical bottle. Lost in her thoughts, she sat as quiet as a star until she heard the beginning of morning's chorus from inside. Da scooped more sea coal into the hearth until the fragrant smoke ribboned out the chimney, winding through bare-limbed trees that towered over the neighborhood. Ma's kettle whistled. Above Mary Margaret, Mr. Bennett's voice called out Mrs. Bennett's name, and the smell of her coffee brewing snaked through the house. Outside was a day full of possibilities, about to begin.

EPILOGUE

Chapter Fifty-Seven

FEBRUARY, 1857, ISLE OF WIGHT, ENGLAND

It had become Bess's custom to go down and meet the afternoon mail boat whenever she was in the village. It never stayed docked for very long, just long enough to drop off the boxes and letters marked for the Isle of Wight.

It had been almost a year since her father was supposed to have returned. Some days in a person's life are so eventful that they remain vivid forever. March 29, 1856, was such a day for Bess—that was when representatives from the Royal Geographical Society had come to Attwood to personally deliver the news to the duke's next-of-kin. Bess remembered that the day they came was a Saturday—overcast with a light drizzle.

"We are so sorry to inform you," they had begun, "that the last time the duke was seen, he was in a carved-out boat with three guides, and they were paddling for their lives downstream while being pursued by a local tribe. The natives were firing what we believe were poisoned arrows from their bows at our men."

"Do you know that he is dead?" Elsie had cried out.

"We do not, Your Grace," the leader of the group had replied. "But no one stayed to try to recover bodies. It would have been a death sentence to go back there and look. Those who did live barely escaped with their lives."

"My papa is a fine swimmer," Bess had blurted out. "He could still be alive."

"It's true, my lady," one of the men answered kindly. "But it is unlikely."

Bess did not give up hope. She would not, although Elsie had started referring to herself as the Dowager Duchess of Kent and wearing black mourning clothes. Bess still waited every day for news that her papa had escaped, and that he had either found his way out or been somehow rescued. She felt certain that he was still alive. There were stories about men being taken by native tribes and held hostage for years. Next month would mark one year since the duke had disappeared. She figured she would be old enough to begin her life as an explorer in a few more years. Certainly Elsie would be delighted to have her out of the house and gone. If her father hadn't returned by then, she was determined to go and bring him home herself.

The postmistress was always there at the Isle of Wight dock to fill her handcart with deliveries before the boat shoved off.

"Anything for us, Mrs. Timpy?" Bess asked as the woman thumbed through the stacks.

The postmistress passed Bess a small stack of letters and a tiny package addressed to Attwood Manor.

Bess quickly skimmed the few letters—nothing important—before turning the package over and examining the markings. The front was addressed to her.

To: Lady Bess Kent
Attwood Manor
Isle of Wight, Great Britain

The neatly printed return address meant nothing to her. It read:

Mr. Hamilton's Pawn and Jewelry Repair Shop.
21 Charles Street.
Boston, Massachusetts.
United States of America

She hurried to escape the windy dock and settled herself inside the Cheeky Cat's Pub, ordering a cup of hot chocolate before carefully unwrapping the package.

She unfolded the note inside that was wrapped around the box and read:

Dear B for Bess,

You'll not believe what I found here in a shop in Boston. I cannot explain it. Fate must have intervened, and now I send it back to you with all the heartfelt affection and gratitude that I have in my soul.

I have no return address for obvious reasons. I know I risk much by even sending you this note. Someday, I can only hope to come back to you and the island I so dearly love.

Devotedly,
H for me.

She flipped the cover off the box and gasped at the sight of her gold cross. How could it be? She barely breathed. She held the back of the necklace closer to the lantern on the table, rubbing her index finger over her mother's engraved initials on the back. Thirteen tiny pearls ran down and across the front—the one in the center missing.

She blinked hard to make out the writing at the bottom of Harry's letter.

P. S.

I may never know how this came to be in Boston, but the pawnshop owner told me that the daughter of the man who sold it to him said that "it was good for something while it was in its power." Marcus Aurelius, right?

P. P. S.

Speaking of Marcus Aurelius, did you ever return those library books you took out for me? I'm sure I cannot afford the late fine I must owe by now.

Chapter Fifty-Eight

Four Years Later

May 5, 1861, Stillwater Plantation, Virginia

She had to be careful. Very careful. Bones moved quickly to make up the guest bedroom. The Yankee visitor had only stayed one night, so there was not much to clean up. She told Queenie that she would have plenty of time to polish up the silver when she was through in the big house. It was already outside on the wooden picnic table, which was covered with newspapers and magazines so the polish wouldn't get all over the table.

For the last month, there was a different kind of tension around the plantation than ever before. Murmurs among the slaves were hopeful that the North was finally going to set them free. Tense conversations between the Brewsters and their friends about a coming war stopped whenever one of the slaves was nearby. Even Mabel was no longer sent off the plantation to do errands.

Every day men on horses would come tearing up the long drive with news for Master Brewster. Old Mistress would always rush out behind her husband to hear what the men had to say. Then the men would gallop off, in a hurry to spread whatever news they had throughout the county.

Bones folded the sheets she'd stripped from the guest bed and looked around. She was alone. She quickly picked up the newspaper the Yankee had left behind and slipped it between the dirty sheets before heading out the door and down the back steps.

"Don't forget to spread papers over the table, girl," Queenie ordered when Bones came in the kitchen house. "Old Mistress got a heap of silver for you to polish up today."

"I already did," Bones said, nodding pleasantly. She was barefoot, slender, and her face was framed by tendrils of dark curls that had sprung loose at her temples.

She slipped the Yankee's newspaper onto the pile to the left of the big black stove. Bones's eyes lit up when she spotted Liza's latest copy of *Merry's Museum Magazine* on the top of the pile. Liza barely bothered to read them anymore.

Bones tucked the polishing paste in one of her apron pockets and piled clean rags on top of the extra

314 〰 *Epilogue* 〰

newspapers she'd gathered to add another layer to the picnic table.

"Make sure you make that silver sparkle," Queenie ordered.

"I will," Bones said. Queenie was moving slower these days. She repeated herself and forgot things. One day she used salt instead of sugar in a peach cobbler. After Old Mistress took one bite, she came storming out to the kitchen house, yelling that Queenie was trying to poison them all. She made poor old Queenie eat a whole bowl of the salty dessert until she gagged.

Bones made sure that the Yankee's newspaper was spread out on the picnic table with its front page faceup. It had been months since she'd been able to sneak a look at the Richmond papers that were delivered with the mail once a week. Lately, as soon as the Brewsters finished reading them, they tossed the papers into the fireplace instead of leaving them for Queenie to use.

Bones carefully read the top lines of the Yankee's paper:

New York Herald, April 13, 1861
THE WAR BEGUN

When she was an old lady, she would tell her grandchildren about this day and how those words jumped right out at her. Hopped straight off that page like a Fourth of July parade.

She was seventeen years old now. The space between her two front teeth had come together nicely, but her feet still jiggled and twitched when she was excited. They were fidgeting so much as she read the paper, her knees kept knocking the bottom of the table.

She could hardly wait till dark, when Mama would be back from the fields, so she could share the information with her. She only wished her granny were still alive to see this glorious day. She had always worried that Granny would die, exhausted, working in the fields. But instead, one night, sitting on their cabin stoop smoking her little pipe, she looked joyfully up at the starry sky she loved and nodded once before her head drooped down onto her chest. Just like that. Mama had said not to grieve too much, because at least now Granny was free.

She finished polishing the coffeepot, and peeled off the top layer of the newspaper to put it in the pile with the dirty papers. Now *Merry's Museum Magazine* lay in front of her. She flipped carefully through the pages.

Bones began to rub slow neat circles over a large sterling-silver tray with vines engraved over the handles when she stopped short at the heading of a story in the magazine.

AGNES MAY AND ME

Bones looked up at the windows to be sure that no one was watching her. When she felt safe, she began reading.

AGNES MAY AND ME
by Mary Margaret Casey

Both our ancestors came straggling over on ships. We have that in common. Mine came willingly, to escape starvation and England's heartless hand. Agnes May's people came stolen from their homes, their ankles and wrists locked in iron cuffs bolted to the ships' floors.

I often try to imagine how her name and the date of her birth came to be tucked into a bottle afloat in the water where it drifted freely with the currents. Why was it I who discovered that moss-draped bottle floating beneath a dark Boston wharf? And I wonder—who is Agnes May, and what is the story behind the bottle and the gold cross necklace engraved with the letters DSS J. K. that shared its journey?

Bones blinked hard and read the last sentence again. *What gold cross?* she wondered. Where else could her bottle have traveled and how did it pick up such a thing? She moved the tray off to the side and spread her arms wide over the paper as she finished reading.

War. Such a tiny little word. It should be longer, loaded as it is with anguish and hope and bitterness and ruthless despair. It should be a word at least a million letters long so that people couldn't say it so easily. So it wouldn't roll off men's tongues so quickly. So when they threatened or declared it, they would have to spend a long, long time considering its bitter, sorrowful results.

But now that war has come, at least let it be worthy. For even with my people's struggles, here in America I own myself. Shouldn't Agnes May and her people at long last be able to say the same?

"Praise the Lord!" Bones cried, forgetting to conceal her joy or the magazine. She wiped her eyes with the back of her hand and read the final notation at the foot of the page.

About the Author: Mary Margaret Casey, age 16, graduates with distinction this spring from the Boston Girls' School.

Author's Note

It is believed that bottles were first placed in the ocean as early as 310 BCE, when the Greeks set them afloat in the Mediterranean Sea to prove that it was formed by the inflowing Atlantic Ocean. The more I read the more I became fascinated by the various reasons people have tossed these little glass messengers into the ocean. Lovelorn sailors in sinking ships threw notes overboard hoping someone would find them and forward them to their loved ones. During one severe storm, even Christopher Columbus placed a report of his discoveries inside a cask along with a note asking that if found, the document be given to Isabella, Queen of Spain. It is intriguing to me to imagine the different reasons a message might be tossed into the water and where the currents might carry it. I always wonder who would find it, and what it would mean to the discoverer.

Around the same time I was finding information about bottles in the ocean, I was also reading several

American slave narratives for the first time. I had thought I was relatively well versed about the American Civil War, but reading these firsthand accounts profoundly affected me. It was just a matter of time before I had written young Bones and figured out that she should toss her name into the James River. Once the Gulf Stream picked up her bottle, I looked at ocean-current charts to figure out where it might land. Then I had to learn about what was happening in that part of the world at that time. And my adventures with researching and writing the interwoven stories of Bones, Bess, and Mary Margaret began.

I tried to stay true to facts even when inventing the lives of my three protagonists. Except for "The Red Sled" in chapter fifty and "Agnes May and Me" in chapter fifty-eight, all the excerpts from *Merry's Museum Magazine* are real—I had great fun reading them in compilation editions. I also read about lonely-hearts advertisements, the summer home of Queen Victoria, British explorations of the Nile River, the American gold rush in California, the potato famine in Ireland, and more. I think many authors live for the moment when a surprising bit of information appears during research. That was the case when I first read that Tiny Tim's illness in Charles Dickens's *A Christ-*

mas Carol has been debated in the most prestigious medical circles for a long time. The consensus is that while people like him were malnourished and could have suffered from rickets, it is most likely that those with symptoms like the character of Tiny Tim actually suffer from a condition called proximal renal tubular acidosis. As in Bridget Casey's case, the condition is serious, but if properly diagnosed is easily treated and quickly cured, even in the 1850s.

Acknowledgments

As I read dozens of books and articles, I quickly learned that research leads to more research. At some point an author has to begin to write. Thank you to my husband, Randy, for putting up with the hundreds of articles, books, and notes that I had stacked around our home at various points during the writing process. Your good humor is, as always, appreciated.

Through GrubStreet, a creative writing center in Boston, I was fortunate to be connected to the talented Ben Winters. His advice about shaping this novel was invaluable.

It was my lucky day when I met a student in a children's literature nonfiction class whom the other students nicknamed "the magic brain." Karen Boss's editorial suggestions and guidance have made this effort far better than it would have been without her. She also made it a heck of a lot of fun.

Finally, thank you to my mother, who convinced me that if I wanted to, I could do anything.

Source Notes

The following references in the text are taken directly from primary-source materials.

On page 14 Bones reads an article and looks at an illustration:

Merry, Robert, Uncle Frank, and Hiram Hatchet, eds. "Africa: Dr. Livingstone's Journeys and Researches in South Africa." *Merry's Museum, Parley's Magazine, Woodworth's Cabinet, and The Schoolfellow 35.* (January–June 1858): 70–73. Reprinted in original format. Lexington, KY: ULAN Press, 2014.

On pages 14 & 15 Bones reads aloud from this article:

Merry, Robert, Uncle Frank, and Hiram Hatchet, eds. "Africa and Its Wonders." *Merry's Museum, Parley's Magazine, Woodworth's Cabinet, and The Schoolfellow 35.* (January–June 1858): 134–36. Reprinted in original format. Lexington, KY: ULAN Press, 2014.

On pages 125 & 126 Bess reads this article in the library:

Merry, Robert, Uncle Frank, and Hiram Hatchet, eds. "The Chinese Wall." *Merry's Museum, Parley's Magazine, Woodworth's Cabinet, and The Schoolfellow 35.* (January–June 1858): 121. Reprinted in original format. Lexington, KY: ULAN Press, 2014.

On page 126 Bess also reads this article:

Goodrich, Samuel. "A Frightened Tiger." *The Youth's Companion.* (July 29, 1869): 234. www.merrycoz.org/yc/TIGER.HTM.

On page 315 Bones reads a newspaper headline:

"The War Begun." *New York Herald*, April 13, 1861, morning edition, front page.

Learn More

In addition to the sources listed in the source notes, I also consulted many others. The following proved especially valuable and instructive. Although some were originally published for adults (those marked with an asterisk), you might find them interesting, too.

BONES

*Gaines, Ernest J. *The Autobiography of Miss Jane Pittman*. New York: Bantam, 1982. First published 1971 by Dial.

*Jacobs, Harriet. *Incidents in the Life of a Slave Girl*. New York: Oxford University Press, 1988. First published 1861 by Thayer & Eldridge.

Lester, Julius. *To Be A Slave*. New York: Puffin Books, 1998. First published 1968 by Dial.

BESS

*Berkeley, Maud. *Maud: The Diary of Maud Berkeley.* Flora Fraser, ed. London: Martin Secker & Warburg, 1985.

Brocklehurst, Ruth. *Usborne History of Britain, The Victorians.* London: Usborne Publishing, 2013.

*Jeal, Tim. *Explorers of the Nile: The Triumph and Tragedy of a Great Victorian Adventure.* New Haven, CT: Yale University Press, 2011.

MARY MARGARET

American Textile History Museum, Lowell, MA. www.athm.org.

Bartoletti, Susan Campbell. *Black Potatoes: The Story of the Great Irish Famine, 1845–1850.* Boston: Houghton Mifflin, 2001.

Nichols House Museum. Boston, MA. www.nicholshousemuseum.org.